The all inclusive guide to Yoga Massage

By José Errol Feria

The All Inclusive Guide to Yoga Massage
Published in the United States by
Enso Circle Media
2370 Market St #155
San Francisco CA 94114
415-552-5524
www.ensocircle.com

First edition published 2010.

Book Design: **Kreaty Ferguson**

ISBN: **978-0-615-38230-2**

Printed in the United States of America

Disclaimer:

The Author of this book is not responsible in any manner whatsoever for any injury that may occur indirectly or directly from the use of this book. Since the physical activities described herein may be too strenuous in nature for some readers to engage in safely, please consult a physician prior to practice.

Dedication

I dedicate this book to my parents, Rose and Evaristo Jr., whose light and love brought me to this world, to my late Lola Cion, who persevered and raised me as a strong, independent thinker, and to my Auntie Sophie and Uncle Art, who supported my family and me in every way they could. I am indebted to them for their unconditional love and generosity.

Also to my Auntie Luz, whose remarkable spirit will always be remembered.

Contents

Tags: yoga, massage, Thai massage, physical, touch, meditation, stress, breath, self, Self, Filipino American culture, military, consciousness, being, emotions, mind, spirituality, aging, relationships, partnerships, immigration, illegal immigrants, future, time, science, engineering, theory of relativity, quantum physics, psychology, philosophy, reality, possibilities

ACKNOWLEDGEMENTS

I thank my yoga and meditation teachers, **Darren Main**, **Michael Alexander**, **Chad Stose**, **Sianna Sherman**, **Darren Rhodes**, **Christina Sell**, **Michael Sebastian** and **Sara Gordon**. Special thanks to **Howard Miller**, *my business coach and mentor* who trusted my work and whose patience I pushed to the limits. My dear clients **Mary Corbett**, **Clare Murphy**, **Peter Kasenenko**, **Tim Gallagher**, **Paul Casagrande**, **Regan Robinson**, **Wade French**, **Vicky Laycock**, and **Carol Music** who have been coming to me for many years and continue to support my work and passion. I love seeing all of you and listening to your life stories – even through touch. My colleagues **Mike Chaplin** *of Sol Gym*, **Susanne Runion** and friends **Paul Wensel**, **Rob Jolin**, **John Hanley**, **Jeannie Zukav**, **Kimby Tan**, **Del Adona** and **Jerry Cox**. My nephew **Erik Estrada**, niece and goddaughter **Pam Estrada**, even in their youth, inspired me to be the best we can. Last but not the least thanks to my cover and interior designer **Kreaty Ferguson** *of Primediart Technologies, illustrators* **Randolph Williams** and **Bradley Golden**, *editors* **Sue Louiseau**, **Tom Bruein** and **Jessica Laycock** for their diligent and visionary works. I share this gift of love with all of you.

Photography by **Steven Underhill.**

Special thanks to **Shoyeido Corporation** for the English translation of all the timeless Japanese Zen quotes.

Warning

Before you begin any strenuous exercise or meditation practice, make sure a health care professional evaluates your condition/s for your own safety and the safety of others—especially if you have medical concerns. Expectant mothers should avoid deep abdomen twists and bends. If you have any questions or difficulty following the poses, consult a yoga instructor or the author.

The techniques and practices in this book can profoundly improve your health and well-being. The fact that you picked up this book most likely means that you are ready to make big changes in your life by getting in touch with your own body and creating balance within yourself, your relationships and work.

INVOCATION

Gayatri Mantra

(Mother of All Mantras and Vedas for Healing)

OM Bhur Bhuvah Svaha

Tat Savitur Varenyam

Bhargo Devasya Dhimahi

*Dhio Yo Nah Prachodayat**

*OM. The primordial energy of the universe.
Permeating through matter, space and time.
That the fabric of light that unites us
With the universal truth and consciousness
Awaken our body and spirit through action and meditation.
We ask for the divine wisdom and enlightenment.
– J. Errol Feria

$E=mc^2$ – Albert Einstein

Introduction

A revelation struck me while washing dishes. It is true that whatever you are doing and wherever you are, there are always opportunities to look inside yourself for reflection. There are no mountains to climb, pilgrimages to holy lands, or gurus to follow in order to attain enlightenment—just you, your Self and the trusty dishwasher.

One morning, I was putting away the bowls I had just hand washed on the dish rack, when two of them rolled over, fell on top of each other and made a loud crashing noise. I got furious. I said to myself, "Fuck!" and thought, "I should have stacked the bowls more carefully; otherwise I could have broken them all." Then the internal conversation went on for two minutes about things I screwed up growing up, all the way back from the time as a kid when I got reprimanded for certain things I did **not** do right. Sympathetically, I caught my train of thought, stopped, turned my mind around, and said to myself, "It's all right. At this moment I am perfectly all right."

There was something revealed about my reaction and thoughts that morning that made me look at other areas in my life where I felt withdrawn. The first thing on my mind was finishing this book after months of setting it aside. At first I couldn't understand why. But nagging thoughts came up like: how hard is it to write or finish a book, and what if I am not good enough, or why am I feeling so vulnerable? Then the aha moment came. Putting away the bowls on the rack or writing this book led me to a future that is based on beliefs—a belief of a **perfect** future that the bowls will behave accordingly without crashing and breaking, or a book that will turn out to be a mega failure. Yikes!

On a path to yogic realization, there is the science called karma yoga[1]. It literally translates, "Union through action." Karma yoga is a way of acting, thinking, and willing, by which you orient yourself toward awareness by acting in accordance with your duty, without consideration of personal, self-centered desires, likes, or dislikes[2]. In short, karma yoga is to act as a way of offering—not due to personal gain. By the way, two of the most famous karma yogis in this century are Mother Theresa and Amma (Mata Amritanandamayi).

In the previous story, the realization of my bruised past and a formidable future caused my present action to shift. The shift made way into an offering. The offering fine-tuned in to the present moment. My paradigm shifted, my mind let go, and new circuits started to develop.

Now, when I wash dishes, I reflect on what is present with my mind and body, freeing every tension that overshadows my light and constricts my creativity. Washing dishes has never been the same for me again. I continued to write—but with more vision, power and humor.
Passion exuded within me, reflecting upon my heart and experiences, while finding an authentic inner voice.
You too may find revelations in your life at this very moment, liberating your trapped mind and actions from routine. Try this for yourself. Breathe deeply. Track the air entering though your nostrils into your lungs. Then slowly exhale through your mouth and say "Ahhh," allowing the muscles on your face, neck, and shoulders to let go. Now breathe deeply again, this time letting the air fill your lungs

[1] From the Bhagavad Gita

[2] Wikipedia

completely until the upper chest lifts up. Slowly exhale through your nose. Now slow down, look into the softness of your heart and listen, and begin to realize what is present, unattached from the past, the future, wants, or personal gain. Feel the warmth, lightness, and openness of your heart and embody a sense of freedom and power. Pause for a moment. Be in this light for a moment.

When you are ready to continue, read the chapters and follow the yoga-massage exercises or meditation practices at the end of each chapter. Let this book be a guide to a dynamic physical and spiritual well-being that is authentic for you. Have this book accessible—to remind yourself that wherever you are and whatever you are doing, there is always that moment to pause for reflection and an offering.

I look forward to sharing these blissful moments with you. Namaste[3].

---

[3] I bow to you.

Who Benefits From This Book

The practice outlined in this book offers numerous benefits and will help you reach many moments of bliss, vitality, and happiness, while avoiding the stress and depletion that usually come with work.

- For couples, it brings them closer together, bonding the relationship with deep meaning and satisfaction.
- For family or community, it promotes harmony and understanding of our collective mind, needs, culture, movement, or action and the world in general.
- For therapists or students, it provides access to new techniques and practices to complement their knowledge and skills, using proper body mechanics and mental discipline, which are so crucial in a successful, healthy career.
- For beginners of yoga, massage, or meditation, it prepares and fertilizes the ground for exploration and growth by getting in touch with their own bodies and others.
- For single men or women, it demonstrates easy-to-follow manual techniques and mind exercises to engage in or overcome fear of touch or intimacy. I have known many single people who met their partners in these yoga massage workshops.
- For parents, it teaches children the beauty, nature, and value of informed touch.

As a note, **always** be respectful of the other person's personal space. Communicating needs and wants is very important. It allows you and the other person to have his or her say on the matter. Learn when to say **no** or that you're feeling uncomfortable. Finally, respect the other person's requests as you would like the other person to respect your own requests.

Allow yourself to learn, open your heart, and discover who you really are. Embody a personal commitment and growth for spiritual well-being—at this very moment. Consider this book an access in reaching your full potential as a human *being*, and not a human *doing*.

What Do I Get Out of this Book?

Let me count the ways.

Besides the many benefits mentioned in the previous section, and asking the question, "What can I give the other person?" it is common to inquire, "What do I **fully** get out of this book?" and "What is this worth to me?"

- With the staggering healthcare costs, and shopping at Walgreens for countless remedies, massage is a sensible way to release tension, unravel knotted muscles, heal sprains and strains, ease acute pain or headaches, and reduce swelling on the joints.

- Save on massage costs and trips to the spa or studio. Stay in the comfort of your own home and play your own relaxing music anytime day or night.

- Make your home your sanctuary and a healing space. Eliminate clutter. Say a mantra: "Less is more".

- Promote family time and "me" time. Turn off the TV or computer for a change, and engage in some social interaction.

- Learning the yoga massage exercises and meditation techniques will prove that giving feels the **same** as receiving.

- Use touch as a gift and tool to connect with other people (and animal companions, too).

- Find the inner healer in you. Tap into energy sources that are way bigger than your own.

- Plug into your own energy and the other person's energy. Dance with them to the beating of your own drums.

- Last but not least, make this work an offering to your higher Self and to others.

How to Use this Book

Every chapter in this book is a modern multi-genre, yet timeless teaching that reveal some of the physical, emotional, and spiritual truths. It illustrates and describes the coming together of two people with easy yoga massage poses and suggests individual meditation practices.

Each step, or body part, is essentially **complete**, and may be practiced each day or each week. It starts off with simple basic moves to acclimate the body to the sensation of touch. Then the physical poses get more advanced, and the meditations get more deeply moving as you progress.

When combined, all 12 poses form a sequence for a full-body-yoga-massage-for-two that usually lasts 90 minutes to two hours. By that time, you may very well have attained a state of bliss. But in reality, be **aware** that bliss can always be instantly manifested in any moment, without requiring a set of steps.

Feel free to jump to any of the steps depending on your current needs. Steps are grouped into three parts or positions of the receiver: prone, supine or seated. Prone is facing down and supine is facing up (on your spine).

There are as many paths to bliss as there are paths to realization. This is one of them. This book is an easy read but deep in meaning. Do remember, paths can sometimes be smooth, rosy or rocky. "Suppose highways were without any bends, just like Roman roads, a one-shot deal straight from New York to Washington, 100 percent straight," said author, teacher and scholar Chogyam Trungpa. The drivers would fall asleep. Because of that, there would be more accidents than if the road had bends in it with road signs here and there. The path is personal experience, and you should take delight in those little things that go on in your lives—the obstacles, seductions, paranoia, depressions, and openness. All kinds of things happen, and that is the content of the journey, which is extremely powerful and important."[4]

For some people, this book is a radical way of thinking and feeling. Be ready to get out of your comfort zones, much like riding a roller coaster. In Howard Miller's book, "You're Full of Shift,"[5] he tells a story about missing the road during an animated conversation with his training partner after weeks of driving to his training site. So they took an uncharted corner. As it turned out, it was a more direct way to where they were going.

He learned three things: one, that they can take chances; two, that they can accept alternatives they've never considered before; and three, how to get comfortable with uncertainty and that it's okay to miss a turn.

---

[4] Trungpa, C, "The Only Way," The Path is the Goal: A Basic Handbook of Buddhist Meditation.

[5] Miller, H, "You're Full of Shift"

The best way to walk a path to realization is to tell a story and the most powerful stories are our own personal stories. See the relevant stories and events in each chapter with your own eyes; hear the sounds as if they're yours. Feel in your bodies and in your own realities the experiences and relationships to these stories. They may or may not be true for you.

Remember, to master, transcend, or transform the self is to know and understand from our direct embodiment or personal experiences.

PROLOGUE

The Sense of Touch

Growing up after the golden era in Manila in the late 1960's, touch was valued and came naturally among close family members.

As kids, we joyfully greeted our elders by taking their hands, slightly bowing in front of them and touching the back of their right hand to our foreheads. We said, "Mano po," which literally means, "your hands please," a respectful way of acknowledging them when we came home from school or following a Sunday mass. In return, they blessed us or patted our heads—or what my grandfather used to do when he visited—he kissed our soft cheeks with his stubbly gray beard wreaking with Old Spice. My "Lola Taba," or rotund grandma, as we call her, however, lightly pinches our cheeks until they're rosy pink and tells us how cute and precious we are. We were her "palangga," or love in Ilongo, uttered in Iloilo's most melodious affectionate dialect. Iloilo is my mother's hometown and my birthplace, located in the Visayas in the central part of the Philippine archipelago. The word "palangga" evokes indescribable tenderness, and takes on a buoyant physical character, "like a caress lovingly bestowed and lovingly received."[6]

Men, in general, shake hands and pat each other on the back, while for women and children—we hug or kiss them on their cheeks once or twice on each side, as a form of greeting. Such social customs, including education, arts, and culture were indicative of 300 years of Spanish colonization. Until the '80's, young men holding hands or showing camaraderie in public were also common in

---

[6] Iloilo, The Rich and Noble Land by Lopez Group Foundation

Manila. In today's even-mixed Filipino and Filipino-American culture, much of that respect, culture, and some traditions are retained and practiced.

Touch, in any given culture, transmits **energy** that—when done with intent—can be either bonding or destructive. This powerful energy can neither be created nor destroyed—it can only be transferred.[7] It is impossible to touch someone without them touching you—both experience giving and receiving at the same time. For example, a hug or reaching for someone's hand is a general gesture of solace or comfort. A mother's or child's warm embrace expresses love and tenderness, while a handshake seals a deal. However, a slap on the wrist, or worse, on the face brings someone back to reality, consequently shaking up a relationship.

The reason we move away from touch may be due to upbringing (cultural), past conditioning (historical), or experience of pain (physical), as a physiological form of a protective mechanism. In effect, we hide our bodies, hearts, heads, foundation, or the "hurt" part of the body underneath the authentic Self.[8] In addition, emotions get shoved deep down, causing us to suffer more.

[7] Law of Conservation of Energy in physics

[8] Self is the big form of self, our divine nature.

Oftentimes, we do not acknowledge the pain as it arises, as if it were something bad, sinful, or a nuisance.
There is an even more common perception, especially among men, that they have to be somehow strong and unmoved by pain and suffering. Such an attitude can often lead to trauma or freezing. When another similar event happens in the future, the experience is replayed again and again, creating a vicious cycle. We get trapped inside our mind and body and out of touch with our being.

When we shift our awareness and release ourselves from this trap, healing begins. The past remains in the past, and we set ourselves free. When we readily accept that our upbringing, beliefs, and experiences are what they are, objectively, without judgment or prejudice, then we can move forward. We move out of our little box and find who we really are—to see, hear, feel, and touch the world in a way we haven't imagined before. It's like driving a car; we do look in the rear view mirror once in a while to see what's behind us, but we mindfully look and drive forward in the direction we want to go.

Re-pairing, as in joining, our body through touch heals our mind, body, and spirit so we become whole and complete again. It reunites all the different parts of our body from top to bottom and from the bottom up, inside and out, paving a direct open path to allow energy to flow freely. It strengthens our core so we feel balanced, centered, and able to stand on our own two feet.

Touch, therefore, becomes a **mutually conscious choice in the present**, not a rule, dogma, or product of the past or the future. It is not an objective but a perfect harmonious relationship with the universal energy that has always been there.

We get to experience touch in a different matrix in the present multi-dimensional moment of possibilities. It grounds us back to Mother Earth, which is our true nature, an offspring of the cosmos. We experience wholeness again "in touch" with our bigger Self, our human "being" and our true Goddess.

History of Yoga Massage

Yoga massage has a rich history and origin from Thai therapeutic massage, also called *nuad boran*. Thai massage dates back before 1830 when the production of ancient epigraphs, statues and relics at the Wat Po temple in Thailand were discovered. Other than these relics, there are no written documents related to the history of Thai massage[9]. Prior to historical data, this practice was handed down through oral traditions and practiced in temples among monks. Later on, they were written, recorded, integrated into the Traditional Thai Medicine (TTM), and then practiced among professionals and laypersons[10].

---

[9] Traditional Thai Medicine: Buddhism, Animism, Ayurveda by C. Pierce Salguero

[10] : A person who does not belong to a particular clergy, group, profession or who is not an expert in some field.

Although Thai massage is related to the classic Indian hatha yoga[11], which dates back some 2,500 years, the practice in itself is unique. In Thai massage, one person moves the other person's body into a particular position and performs manual manipulations of the spine, joints, and muscles to energize the body, and improve flexibility and strength. A balanced state of mind, focused concentration, and sharp memory also result from the work. **Both** practitioners assume simple restorative yoga poses while one person is doing the massage.

In addition to the physical characteristic of hatha yoga poses, there is also the subtle energetic aspect to take into consideration that eases the flow of energy throughout the body. The theory is that the body has 72,000 *sen* lines or vessels in which *lom or* energy travels through the body. The *sen* lines are treated with pressure points using the

[11] Hatha means force or determined effort because the path of hatha yoga demanded rigorous discipline. Hatha Yoga Pradipika Sutra is an approach towards liberation written by Swatmarama. (B.K.S. Iyengar, Light on Yoga.)

thumbs or the palm of the hand. These lines are similar to the meridians in Traditional Chinese Medicine and acupressure. Think of the *sen* lines or meridians as the electrical wiring in your house, whereby a switch or dimmer controls the flow of current to different appliances or lighting in every room.

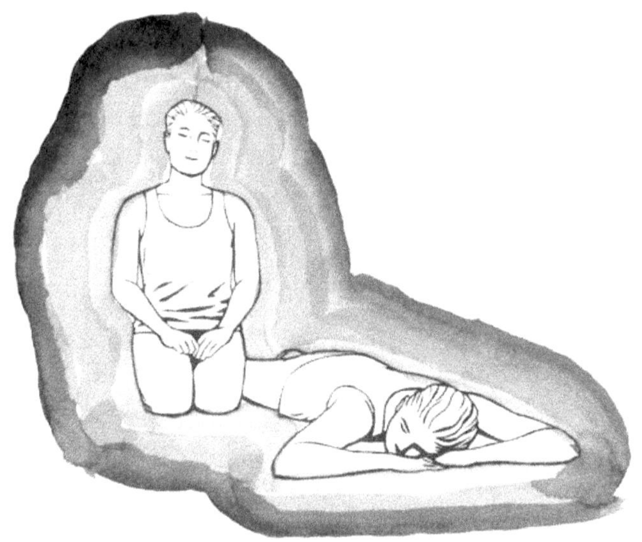

Figure A

Another characteristic that makes Thai massage unique is the spiritual practice of Buddhism and Tantra[12] yoga. According to their philosophy, our being is made up of five layers of energetic bodies (*see fig. A*). Generally, the first layer is the physical body, which is made up of matter and particles. Second is the energy body or the layer of life force just above the skin—some people call it the aura. The third layer is the mental body, where thoughts, cognition, and will are experienced. Fourth is the ego, which provides one's identity or one's definition of self. The fifth and last

---

[12] Tantra philosophy is the basis of Buddhism and yoga.

layer is the blissful body that allows one to connect with the metaphysical world.

Obstruction of the free flow of energy results in an insufficient supply of *prana*, or vital energy to the body. This loss or insufficient supply of *prana* could lead to mental, physical, and spiritual imbalances in the different bodies, which may be manifested in the form of dis-ease, discomfort and emotional imbalance.[13] Our aim is to open the obstructions, allowing energy to flow freely. Through awareness, yoga, massage, and meditation, we return to a blissful natural state.

[13] Thai Yoga Massage, Kam Thye Chow

Yoga in its true essence literally means yoke or union in Sanskrit—the union of body, mind and spirit. A yoke traditionally is a wooden bar or frame by which two farm animals are joined at the heads or necks so they can work together. Many people associate yoga with the physical poses of stretching (asana), breathing (pranayama) and meditation (dhyana) or spirituality, but it is more of a comprehensive practice, as Darren Main emphasized in his book *Yoga and the Path of the Urban Mystic*. He writes, "Yoga is a practice, not perfection. It's the process of returning to your practice over and over again that gives you the benefits. Doing the perfect yoga pose or clearing your mind of all thought is all well and good, but in the end it is the practice of returning to yoga that allows you to live life to the fullest."[14]

[14] Main, D., *Yoga and the Path of the Urban Mystic*

Figure B

Within the five energetic bodies that shroud the physical body,[15] there are also seven major chakras or wheels like vortices of energies that spin along the length of the spine, according to Tantric and yogic philosophy (*see Fig. B*). These major chakras are best described in *Table 1*.

The wheels or vortices in a chakra spin in different directions from chakra to chakra. For example, the first or root chakra spins in a clockwise direction for the giver, and counter clockwise for the receiver, thus enabling the partners to complement each other's energies. The

[15] See Fig A.

clockwise rotation carries the "male"[16] dominant characteristic or *yang* nature in the Chinese teaching. The counter clockwise rotation carries the "female"[17] receptive characteristic or *yin* nature. The rotations alternate as the vortices move up the spine all the way to the center of the top of the head.

It is **not** so important to know how the direction of the chakra is moving as it is to have awareness that there is a subtle energy that complements or highlights each person's energy. Also, at any given moment, the wheels switch directions by themselves like a dance of energies or the ebb and flow of the river.

---

[16] I quoted male and female nouns here because socially and physiologically, we are divided into male and female groups. However, on a cellular and transcendental level, we are all one of the same and switch gender roles depending on the circumstances.

[17] See footnote 13.

Chakra	Name	Location and Function
1st chakra	Root center or base	Base of spine between anus and genitals, connected to coccyx. Energy opens downward to the ground. Identifies survival and connection with Mother Earth.
2nd chakra	Sacral	Lower abdomen, upper part of sacrum, approximately at upper limit of pubic hair. Links with emotions and sexuality.
3rd chakra	Solar plexus	Two fingers above the navel. Controls power and will.
4th chakra	Heart	Just above the sternum, center of chest (breastbone). Equates to love and balance.
5th chakra	Neck or throat	Throat, between inner collarbone and larynx. Associated with communication and creativity.
6th chakra	Brow or third eye	Center of forehead, one finger above the nose center or forehead, approx. two fingers deep in head. Connects with intuition and imagination.
7th chakra	Crown	Center of top of head. Energy opens upward to the skies. Parallels knowledge, understanding and connection with the cosmos.

Table 1.[18]

[18] Sharamon, S and Baginski, B; The Chakra Handbook

Preparing for Your Journey

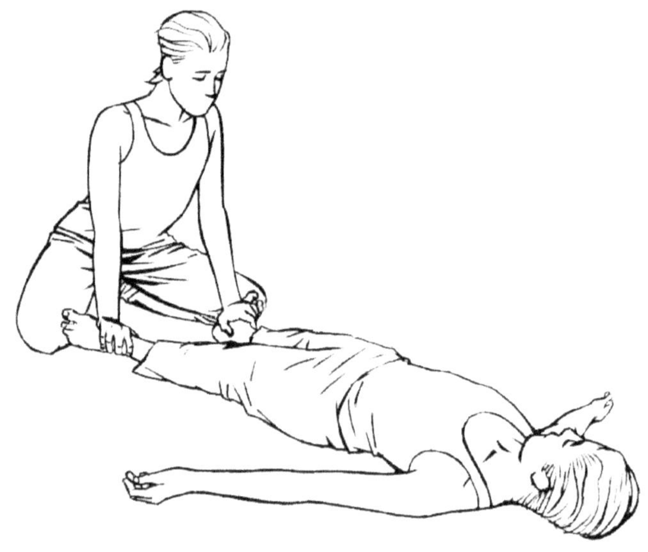

Have you ever gone on a trip you've been anticipating only to find out at the airport that your passport had expired (it happened to a good friend of mine), or realized that you left the iron on? Well, preparation is key to smooth sailing. Here's how:

1. Find a quiet, warm, comfortable place away from electrical appliances, including cell phones that can interfere with your own energy.
2. You may play soft soothing music in the background or listen to the outside natural sound of rain, water, wind, or the ocean, if available.
3. You need a firm mat big enough for your partner to lie on and for you to move around with ease. Folded blankets, comforters, natural fur, two yoga mats placed together, a firm king or queen size bed may also be used.

4. You might want to light some candles, scented oils, incense, or the fireplace to add a full sensory experience.
5. Set a "date"—a time for the two of you to come together and create your own world.
6. If any of these preparations tend to disrupt your intent to come together, then by all means, get into the poses directly. These are just options for you to consider. Lightly pack your bags and enjoy the adventure.

Preparing for Meditation

For individual meditation, find a quiet, warm, comfortable place, again away from electrical appliances, including cell phones that can interfere with your own energy. Start by meditating for 10-15 minutes each day, gradually increasing the time to 60 minutes as you get used to training your mind. Be patient. Remember, meditation is a lifelong practice so I suggest you slow down, smell the roses, and experience your thoughts along the way. Observe where you're thoughts take you—but do not follow them. Track your mind as it wanders away without you going away with it. Just be the observer of your own thoughts, like a fly on the wall.

Be patient. The caveat to this practice is that there is no destination to this path. You end up exactly where you are. Focus on your breathing. Notice the rise and fall of your chest and abdomen. When you catch your mind wandering, refocus on your breathing.

Some people meditate for days, or in a group, either guided or silent. I highly recommend visiting a Zen Center near you or Spirit Rock located in Marin County, north of San Francisco. You may also look for a local meditation teacher.

Meditation instructions in the book are written for individual practice unless otherwise noted.

Sit on a mat or meditation cushion in an easy cross-legged position. You may also use a chair but make sure it is not so comfortable that you might fall asleep. (Sleeping through meditation means you followed your thought of sleepiness.) Padding the feet with a low pillow or mat is good to ease low back tension.

This page is left blank intentionally. You may write your insights and observations on this page or a piece of paper.

PART ONE

PRONE: EMBRACING MOTHER EARTH

This page is left blank intentionally. You may write your insights and observations on this page or a piece of paper.

CHAPTER ONE

AS ABOVE SO BELOW

*"In the mind that is not attached to anything—happiness dwells. Once we remove the barriers that surround our own self, everything will merge with the source, which we really are. A clinging thought, however, can cause doubts, jealousies and conflicts. Tears of misery overwhelm us, if we forget the feeling of appreciation for all we have already been given." –**Japanese proverb***

This initial step taps our body to an expansive and unlimited source of energy in two ways: 1.) Energy within, and 2.) Energy without. We tap energy internally within us through deep breathing called **inspiration**. The Merriam-Webster dictionary defines inspiration as the elevation of creativity or intellect, the arousal of the mind and emotions, or communication with the divine truth. We breathe deep by inhaling through the nose and allowing the lower part of the lungs to fill first and then allowing the upper lungs to get completely filled with air. (Remember, your lungs extend to the bottom of your rib cage.) We then slowly exhale all the air from the upper to the lower lungs. The air we breathe provides essential nutrient oxygen into the cells. Therefore, shallow breathing suffocates the cells, making the muscles, connective tissues, and viscera feel less energized and more stressed.

The second expansive source of energy comes from an outside source: Mother Earth or Mother Nature, the sun and the universe. In this particular pose, we are closer to Mother as we sit directly on the ground. We energetically root the base of our spine, also referred to as the first chakra,[19] to her core. (In a sense, this is an example of why the first chakra opens downward to the ground.) Draw this energy up and allow it to enter through the tailbone. Then move this steady stream of energy along the length of the spinal column.

Now find your ground just like a tall erect poplar or oak tree; root yourself firmly to the ground, gathering warmth, support, and power from that deep energetic force. Expand and radiate this focal energy throughout the body like branches and leaves on a tree all the way through your fingertips and outside your skin creating ripples of energy and glow around you.

---

[19] Chakra in Sanskrit means wheel, a phenomenon where energy pools swirl along the body. There are seven major chakras up and down the spine and hundreds of minor ones. Chakras are discussed in more detail in the section, Demystifying the Chakras.

So here in step one, we are bridging a connection from our own primary physical material body to our secondary subtle energetic body. Practice this step faithfully and feel the natural lightness in your own body arise.

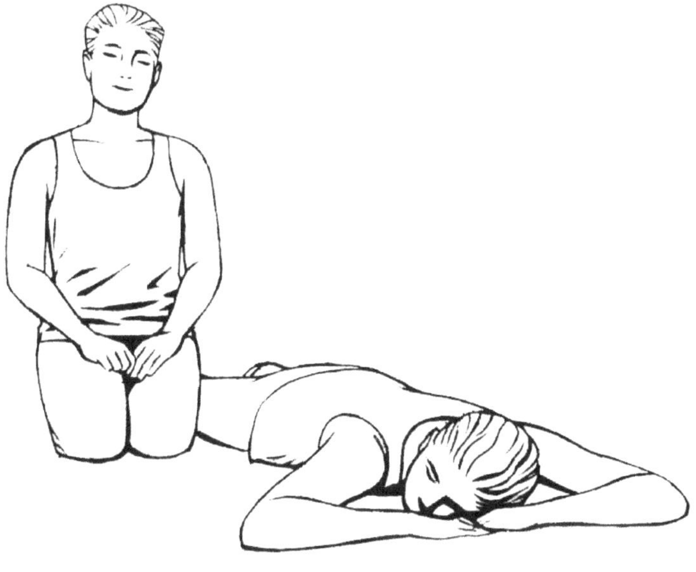

Figure 1

Hot Yoga Tip!

Hero pose is an easy sitting position with thighs parallel to the lower legs and on the floor. Tops of feet flat on the floor, big toes touching each other. You may use a folded blanket under the feet or between thighs and legs for comfort.

Partner Yoga Instructions:

1. Giver sits on both heels in hero pose close to partner's right torso facing the head (see Fig 1). Pause for a moment and take a few deep breaths.
2. Move to face your partner.
3. Place one hand on your partner's low back and the other behind the heart. Note that once you touch your partner, your intention is to remain in contact with him or her until the end of the sequence, or for the most part.
4. Synch with your partner's heart beat and draw in energy through deep breathing or from your connection between the root or base chakra and Mother Earth, whichever is appropriate for you.
5. Then radiate this energy all throughout your body from the head to the fingertips.
6. Be present at this point, and mentally prepare yourself to give **and receive unconditional loving kindness** or **offering**.
7. Find a deep connection between you and your partner. You may reach a deep meditative state as you move along the steps.

A REPLANT

Let us begin our story with a separation. I saw the world from the eyes of a child coming from poor and undereducated parents in Manila. At the age of three, my grandmother from my father's side, and her two children from her second marriage (my aunt and uncle), took me from my parents. With their good intentions, they raised my sister and me until adulthood. My grandmother was a retired pharmacist, while my aunt and uncle were middle-class working professionals. A year after I graduated from the University of Santo Tomas, with an engineering degree in hand, I joined the U.S. Navy and got transferred to San Diego, California, for basic military training.

At the age of 23, I found myself separated from my roots, and family once more, this time 7,000 miles across the Pacific. But because of my incessant curiosity of the world, sense of adventure, and the excitement of the unknown, I adapted well and thrived in the "American" culture. There must have been an underlying reason for me to uproot myself, explore and share myself with people I encountered and served. Five years later, I established a permanent residence in San Francisco.

What I love about the "city by the bay" is the melting pot of people, culture, food, art, science, philosophy, politics, and religion. I have access to almost anything here. The city is diverse, colorful, cutting edge, and has been recognized as the Paris of the West since the early 20th century. She's become a fertile ground for me to re-establish my roots and flourish in this entangled universe, important for my survival, growth, and security. Not all these come at an easy price though, as I've been through many storms in my life. However, I stayed deeply grounded, adapted, and swayed with the strong winds of change that came my way.

Who I've become now is an embodiment of different cultures, education, religions, observations, discoveries, travels, and meditations. They say you are what you eat. But no matter how diverse our life is, or has become, we all come from the same source of power and energy, the same building blocks of our entire being, following a path on this planet we call earth.

We all have different backgrounds, different beliefs, and most of us migrate from different states or countries. With modern technology to connect our worlds closer, we find that our thoughts and the same technology separate us from one another. Let us be reminded that we are all one; we need this connectedness, and we are all in this one world together.

MEDITATION PRACTICE: SINKING INTO THE SOFT GROUND

For both giver and receiver:

1. Receiver lies face down, the perfect receptive position to ground yourself of all energy, positive and negative, back to Mother earth.
2. Synch with the earth and the universe's heartbeat.
3. Close your eyes.
4. Gather all tension from your body starting from the top of your head, forehead, throat, heart, lungs, sacrum, and groin all the way to the bottom of your feet.
5. Imagine this mass of energy melting into the ground and going deep into the earth.
6. Now feel the union and deep connection with her, surrendering all your thoughts, tensions and fears.
7. Pause.
8. Giver sit close to the receiver, draw energy from the ground up and channel yourself with the source rising.
9. Come together powerfully with your partner, like the yin-yang energy[20]—whole, complete, centered and balanced.
10. Breathe deeply.
11. Stay with this pose until you feel a sense of fullness. Stay sustained. Stay connected. Then move on to the next pose when you're ready.

---

[20] Yin-yang, in Chinese philosophy is the complementary opposites within the greater whole.

This page is left blank intentionally. You may write your insights and observations on this page or a piece of paper.

CHAPTER TWO

BREATHING FROM YOUR BACK BODY

"May the universe help us—understanding the way of the source is a difficult challenge." – ***a Japanese quote***

This next pose prepares the receiver's body to welcome the giver, who now channels energy from a universal source. By unblocking energy along the back muscles and spine, we are allowing a direct path of least resistance for energy to flow smoothly. We carry a lot of tension or knots along our back muscles, evidently by sitting in front of the computer for long hours, attending to our families, or working as caregivers. Soothing firm strokes along the back allow energy to move to the rest of the body just like opening small dams along a river. It also assures your partner, who is now in a passive receptive position that he or she is in a safe comfortable place and is taken care of.

Figure 2

Hot Yoga Tip!

Kneeling pose is a precursor to a runner's thigh stretch. Bend one knee with the top of the foot on the ground. The other knee is bent exactly 90 degrees; both second toes on the feet are in line with the heels and knees to prevent injuring the kneecaps and ankles. Hug legs actively to the midline to maintain balance and stability.

Partner Yoga Instructions:

1. Giver straddle partner's low back in kneeling pose, one knee on the ground for support (see Fig 2). Maintain a relaxed posture by supporting your low back, keeping it straight, your abdomen tight, and medial shoulder blades slightly squeezed together (about 10%).
2. Place both palms on partner's low back. Slowly walk hands along the back muscles simultaneously toward the shoulders and then back down to the low back.
3. Work with the breath. Repeat twice.
4. Alternative move: starting from the low back, move hands alternately toward the shoulders and back down.
5. Stretch the shoulders and back by anchoring one hand firmly on the pelvis and pressing on the opposite shoulder towards the head with the other hand. Avoid pressing directly down on the bones, as it might feel uncomfortable.

Figure 3

For a deeper move:

1. Move to the side of your partner and place supported thumb (thumb over closed fist) or thumb over thumb (see Fig 3) over low back muscles and move up along the side of the spine. Note: pressure is generated more on the upper rather than the lower thumb. Bottom thumb should stay passive and relaxed.
2. Advanced move: Straddle your partner and use the fleshy part of your forearm perpendicular to the length of the back muscles to apply pressure. Make sure not to put pressure directly on the spine. Use your whole body and not your arms to transfer pressure. Relax the whole arm while performing this move.
3. Remember as you move through these steps to keep your back straight and relaxed. Feel the energy move through your own body as if you are receiving or mirroring the work yourself. Effortless giving and unconditional love comes with practice.

THE BATTERED CHILD

I worked on a female client who complained about a spasm on her low back. She told me that it had been bothering her for a while, and felt worse when she heard the little girl next door crying. Here in the hills of San Francisco, the homes built in the 1920's are situated right next to each other, so that sound goes easily through the walls and windows depending on the wind direction. She said that she was familiar with such crying because her father physically abused her when she was a little girl, while her mother did nothing to stop it. Responding to the next-door-neighbor girl's cry, my client immediately notified the authorities to report the incident. At that point that's all she could do to help.

I started to work and placed my hands on my client's back and noticed major tension in her upper and lower spine. These areas correspond to the back of her heart and abdomen. I asked her to open her heart even more to allow the energy she's been holding to release through her wide-open heart as I massaged her upper back. She then burst into tears and started to spontaneously pray for the little girl's safety.

The whole time, I channeled a path and held a space for her to allow a release of emotions and physical tensions that manifested in her whole body. She embodied her own fear and suffering through vibration, sound, and prayer as she eased toward her own healing—her own security and safety. This is called an "emotional release," and it sometimes happens during a massage session. It is powerful healing for the client as well as humbling for the massage practitioner.

(Keep in mind that I am a licensed massage therapist and not a psychotherapist. Such events are uncommon and outside the scope of my work. However, these incidents do unfold occasionally on the massage table. As a professional I need to know how to act accordingly or refer my clients to other professionals as necessary.)

The best we can do for our friends, family, and clients who come to us for help is to have compassion, hold space for clearing, and just listen. They will naturally heal when they are ready to heal. Our minds and bodies have an innate ability to heal themselves. Our job as caregivers is to be the mirror of our friends, family, or client's health or suffering. We can be the light to other people as they can be the light for us.

MEDITATION PRACTICE: MANTRA MEDITATION

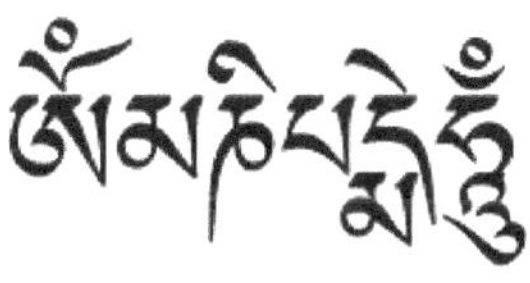

OM Mani Padme Hum

Recite a mantra[21] if the mind remains restless. The mantra's energy carries the union of sound and moving vibrations. Listen to the ring of a bell, or the sound of silence in nature without giving it meaning, but simply the manifestation of pure sound experienced with its emptiness.

Through mantra meditation, we are able to separate our attachment to words, speech, and sound stored in our memories. We experience sound as essentially empty whereas hearing modulates into pure listening. Physiologically, mantra energy produces vibrations in the body that help and correct the functioning of all the glandular and cellular systems like the soothing melody of a lullaby.

The most recited Sanskrit[22] mantra is *OM mani padme hum*, especially revered by the devotees of the Dalai Lama, the spiritual leader of Tibet. It is the mantra for compassion. Numerous translations include jewel lotus or wisdom purity. My favorite one was given by my Anusara[23] yoga teacher Sianna Sherman. She said, "It is the pure spiritual

---

[21] A mantra is akin to a prayer or an invocation

[22] Sanskrit is the classical language of India, considered sacred and divine.

[23] Anusara yoga is a school and philosophy founded by John Friend.

awakening of one's self, unfolding as the lotus flower, deeply rooted in the mire of our human nature."

But then again, these translations carry no attachments—only the pure mantra and beauty of sound and energy.

1. Sit comfortably and say A-U-M. Open your mouth wide and say "AHH," followed by "OOH," then finish with "MMM." Aum is the primordial sound of the universe. All existence—human, animal and plants, respond to sound and vibration. Our sense of hearing attunes us with this true nature.
2. Take a hike in the wilderness and listen to the "a-u-m" **hum** of nature. Translate Aum with "I am" and physically own this energy. (Notice how Aum, hum, and "I am" rhyme with one another as they carry the same vibratory energy).
3. Recite a mantra, prayer, invocation, psalm, or affirmation of your own.

Repeat a mantra 9 to 108[24] times, using mala[25] beads or a rosary, if you have one, until you experience high resonance into each cell and space of your whole body. This is the level when your body leaves its physical state and becomes one with the pure energy—the Aum, hum and "I am" of the universe.

---

[24] These are auspicious numbers in the Buddhist tradition.

[25] Mala beads are prayer beads used by Hindus, Buddhists and practitioners.

CHAPTER THREE

HEART TO HEART

"When spring comes, the sprouts of wild grasses appear from the ground by themselves—the sprouts trust the earth." – ***a Japanese proverb***

This is a powerful pose that complements the work we previously performed through opening the back channel. The heart chakra collapses or freezes when we are under pressure, stress or in fear. You have probably heard of the flight or fight response, a natural protection mechanism for real or perceived dangers. Our entire body forms a human "shield" to protect the most vital organs of our body.

Exposing our heart center, one might say, makes us even more vulnerable to danger. On the other hand, it makes us human and resilient as a person. Beaming our heart to other people and the world also gives us freedom and a sense of warmth, kindness, and softness. We are innately capable of facing the challenges of the world and what it presents, and it teaches us—if we only allow our hearts to open.

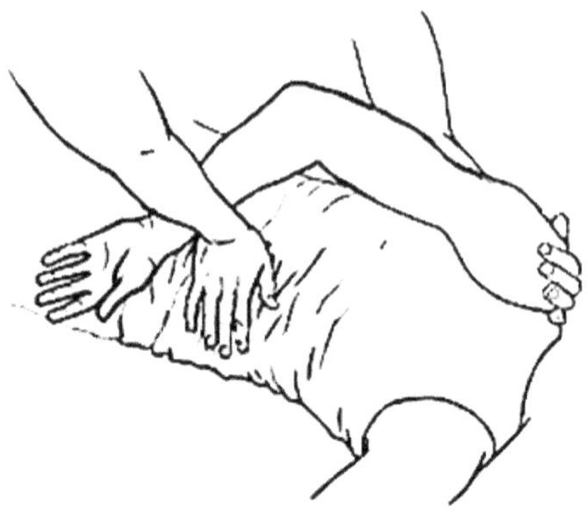

Figure 4

Hot Yoga Pose:

Low cobra pose. Lie facing down, legs firmly pressed and rooted on the ground. Place hands palms down, directly underneath the shoulders. Inhale. Press the floor as you lift your chest and upper body up. Prevent low back strain by keeping your legs firmly on the floor with a slight internal rotation of the thighs and engaging the abdomen muscles. Exhale.

Partner Yoga Instructions:

1. Giver straddles partner's low back with one knee on the ground keeping the low back straight and the abdomen tight. Bring partner's hand behind his or her low back, if possible.
2. Scoop partner's shoulders with outside of hands, squeeze the shoulder blades together, rise up and open partner's shoulder and the center of the heart off to the side (Fig 4).
3. Rotate shoulder both ways twice.
4. Use your free elbow to gently press on the area between the spine and shoulder blade.
5. Repeat on the other shoulder.

6. Receiver interlaces fingers behind neck and squeezes shoulder blades together. Giver scoops both hands under partner's armpits.
7. Giver slowly pulls partner's shoulder and peels upper back off the floor into a low cobra pose. Giver leans back, holds the pose for a few seconds, and then returns to neutral.
8. Make sure both giver and receiver's abdomens are engaged while holding this pose to maintain balance, stability and strength.
9. Repeat twice.

Figure 5

<u>**Caution:**</u> Proceed with this step only if you and your partner are comfortable with your low back and leg strength.

1. Cross partner's hands in front of his or her chest.
2. Grab one forearm (avoid wrist joint) from underneath, step in between partner's legs, brace yourself and **gently** twist partner's torso by pulling straight back (*see Fig 5*).
3. Make sure giver's low back is strongly supported by the legs, bracing the low back by tightening the abdomen muscles. Squeeze the shoulders together keeping them back, low and relaxed.

An Empty Canvas

Changing careers could be one of the most stressful times in one's life. We fear for the future and want to hold on to the past.

In 2001, during the dot-com bust era, our company announced a huge restructuring. Fortunately, or unfortunately, in my case, I was one of the employees they retained. At that point in my career, I felt ready to move on after years of working as an engineer for a high tech firm. I stormed into my manager's office that afternoon and volunteered to get laid off, much to his and my surprise. The challenge ahead of me seemed to be more interesting than the stress, boredom, and depression I suffered at that time.

As soon as I left the company I let out a sigh of relief and experienced a sense of freedom that I had been longing for. I realized I could do whatever I want for the rest of my life from that day on. Weeks later, after meeting an acquaintance who went to massage school in the east bay, I found my way to the National Holistic Institute in Emeryville and signed up for their 11-month Massage Therapy and Health Educator Program.

The back-to-school anxiety and learning human sciences had me worried at first. There was also a huge financial and time commitment involved. However, in the end, as if it was my true nature, I began to love the course and learned to help people with their own healing—including mine.
It gave me great pleasure and satisfaction to know that I made a difference in someone's life at the end of each day. I felt empowered, stimulated, and self-expressed.

The lesson I learned was that no matter how challenging things are, I remained true to myself, had fun, and followed my heart. In the words of Paramahansa Yogananda, "If you want to be sad, no one in the world can make you happy. But if you make up your mind to be happy, no one and nothing on earth can take that happiness from you."[26]

In uncertain times like we are in right now, look at life as an opportunity for growth. Count your blessings. There are reasons why things happen the way they do—you will find out in retrospect. It's like when you are in the water, you cannot see the ocean. But when you take yourself away from the water you see the vastness of the world.

One of the prayers I learned from my Reiki[27] *sensei*[28] from the Usui tradition is:

I give thanks for my many blessings
Just for today I will not anger[29]
Just for today I will not worry
I will do my work honestly
I will be kind to people and every living thing.

---

[26] Yogananda, P., *How to Be Happy All the Time*

[27] Reiki is a form of energy healing originated in Japan by Dr Mikao Usui by the laying of the hands

[28] Sensei means teacher in Japanese

[29] This is the exact syntax the original prayer was translated from Japanese

MEDITATION PRACTICE: DROPPING THE LIGHT INTO THE CHANNEL

1. Gather all your thoughts from the back of your head and bring them to the front lobe or prefrontal cortex of the brain, where the will and the third eye chakra reside.
2. Now condense your thoughts as a concentrated beam of laser light.
3. Drop this fine light into your heart.
4. Allow this light to brighten and expand your heart, making it more open and spacious.
5. Feel what is manifesting inside your heart, whether it's warmth, comfort, openness, or any feelings you feel are true for you.
6. If deep emotions occur allow your heart to open even more.
7. Imagine your heart expanding as big as the room you are in, or the house, the city, the country, the world, or the universe.
8. Now open your eyes and see what's in front of you, as if looking into a mirror. This is the reflection of your true being. A reflection of your Self.
9. How you see the world is the light that is inside you. You begin to see others as part of yourself and love others, not judge them. What you do to build or heal others is the same as you do to yourself.[30]

[30] I acknowledge and thank my meditation teacher Michael Sebastian for sharing this practice.

This page is left blank intentionally. You may write your insights and observations on this page or a piece of paper.

CHAPTER FOUR

BUILDING TRUST: KNEES TO GLUTS

"A monk is walking through a snowstorm on a freezing country road. A strong will gives us courage and the help to forget our difficulties." – ***A Japanese saying***

Taking calculated risks is one of the keys in giving an effective massage. We would like to give the perfect amount of pressure to please our partner. But there are times that we don't know our partner's pain tolerance or threshold on any given part of the body, or at a period of time, so we end up hurting them. It can be unnerving. Just be aware that every part of the body responds to stimulus differently. This is one of the poses that can be very rewarding if done with care. It only takes a little practice. Trust is important in all relationships. The more you practice and become consistent in your action, the more the other person has trust in you.

Figure_6

Hot Yoga Tip:

Cat and cow poses. Get on your hands and knees, hands under the shoulders pressing firmly on the ground and knees slightly wider than hip width apart. Exhale, round and curve the spine towards the ceiling, release head towards the floor, like a scared cat, keeping the abdominal muscles engaged. Inhale, do the opposite, tailbone and chest towards the floor and head facing forward, releasing and rounding the abdomen and back kidney area. Repeat two to three times.

Yoga Massage Instructions:

1. Giver plants one knee at a time to partner's glut muscles along the top bikini line (*see Fig 6*). Avoid the middle part of the gluts between the mid sacrum and the hip joint because the sciatic nerve runs along this area. Ask your partner for feedback.
2. Giver swings his or her feet on top of partner's hind legs in table position.
3. Giver palms back muscles starting from the lower to the upper back. Giver can assume the cat and cow poses as he slowly moves along the back muscles.
4. Alternate move: Giver grabs partner's forearm (avoid the wrists as they can be sensitive) into a cobra pose, as demonstrated in Figure 6. Make sure you're both in a stable position before you execute this. Play around with it.
5. Alternate move: Giver can move knees in a slow circular pattern to knead partner's glut muscles.

The Way the Water Flows

When I started doing yoga massage workshops I laid out a plan gathering all the teaching materials, selecting basic poses to teach as a foundation, rehearsing the two-hour class over and over again, reserving the room, preparing the marketing materials, distributing them, inviting people, etc. I mean lots of preparation needs to be done in the beginning.

Then I asked myself: Are people going to come? Of course some signed up, but there was no way for me to find out until the day of the workshop how many people were actually going to show up. I just had to trust that what I sowed on fertile soil would sprout into something fruitful.

Surprisingly, I had a great turnout on the first day with 14 students. I did have one workshop months later where I had one student. That time was very rewarding because we had fun. I put my undivided attention into this one lucky student.

Who really determines the outcome after you've done your duty? There's only so much we can and cannot control in our lives.

Take into consideration Japanese scientist Dr Masaru Emoto's experiment on water molecules and how thoughts, words, and feelings impact the earth and our health. What he discovered was that water from crystal springs and water that has been exposed and crystallized to loving words or music like "Thank You," "Loving Chi," "You're Beautiful," or Mozart's Symphony No 40, produced brilliant, complex and colorful snowflake patterns. In contrast, polluted water or water exposed to negative words, like "I Hate You," "You Make Me Sick," or "I Will Kill You," formed incomplete, chaotic, asymmetrical, and sinister looking patterns.[31]

Since our body consists mostly of water, imagine how these thoughts, words, and feelings affect our own bodies, other people, living things, and nature. How much power does intent have in our lives, really?

[31] Dr Emoto, M: *The Hidden Messages in Water*

Meditation Practice: Active Sitting Meditation

Sitting during meditation can be a challenge for most people. Even those who meditate for years have the sensation of tightness in their low backs, knees, and hips. Whether you sit cross-legged on a mat or sit regularly on a chair, there are specific active muscle engagements to prevent or relieve muscular strain so you can tune in fully.

1. First, you might consider using a pillow under your sits bone.
2. Next, separate the fleshy gluteus (ass) muscles so you're rooted on your sits bones, planting yourself firmly on the ground.
3. Internally rotate the thighs toward the back of the body along the length of the thighs from the sits bones to the top of the knee. This motion will tend to stick the tailbone out.
4. Counter this motion by tilting the tailbone toward the front of the body, lengthening the low back and making you sit up straight.
5. Actively engage your inner thighs and tailbone to support your upper body.
6. Meditate on the mechanics of sitting and see how this may deepen your practice and save your own back.

CHAPTER FIVE

PELVIC WARM UPS

"External reminders and self-discipline are important aspects of Zen practice. A wise teacher knows the essence of both." – ***a Japanese saying***

As our work gets deeper into the body we need to remember what the foundation and the core of our work is based upon. Warming up before we begin a new section is always a good practice. The pelvic area especially needs lots of attention because tension, shame, and guilt originate there. It's also an area where many men and women feel vulnerability because of its close proximity to the sexual organs. This pose helps us get back to our primal state and be comfortable with our own sensual bodies.

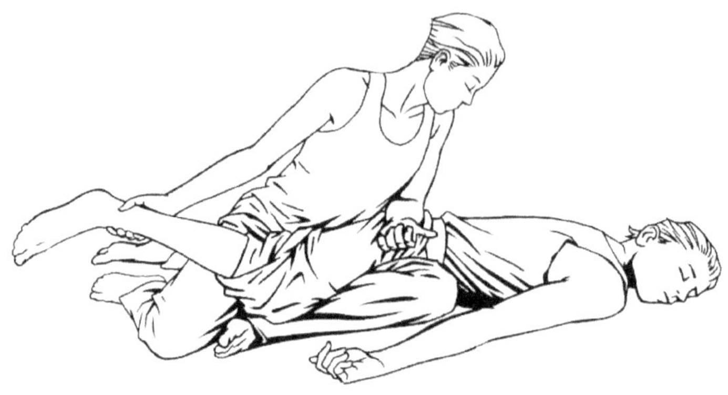

Figure 7

Yoga Massage Instructions:

1. Giver sits next to partner's right hipbone facing the head.
2. Giver grabs partner's right heel with the left hand and draws the heel close to the gluts stretching the quad muscles.
3. Rotate hip joint by moving the ankle in a circular motion. Try moving from small to big circles in both clockwise and counterclockwise directions.
4. Alternative move: Press the right palm over the hip joint giving it a firm traction as you move the hip joint.
5. Lift partner's right leg and slide under so your thigh facing your partner is now under his or her hip crease (*see Fig 7*).
6. Use the fleshy part of your relaxed forearm to massage the thighs and gluts.

Foot Soldiers

Traveling can be hard on the body—especially on the hips, because of the amount of walking on uneven road surfaces, whether it is dirt, grass, cobblestones, concrete, or ice. A female client came in for a massage session after a trip from Madrid. She said she enjoyed her vacation except that the roads she walked on were all uneven. Her hips had to adjust to the changes on the road as she walked for hours exploring the city. My advice to her was to do stretches every once in a while to reset and realign her joints and exercises in the mornings to warm up the pelvic and hip muscles. Traveling can sometimes take a toll on our body. We get used to the paths we walk on daily. So once we go outside our usual path, our body gets disoriented. Flexibility is important to adapt ourselves to the changing external environment.

We also go through emotional paths that can be shocking to our nervous system. After four and a half years in the U.S. Navy, and having been deployed twice to the Persian Gulf during war, my enlistment ended. I was sent back to the Philippines with an honorable discharge. According to immigration laws then, U.S. citizenship was not an option regardless of my military service unless I married an American citizen. So I returned to Manila and used my GI Bill to get an MBA degree at De La Salle University while I planned my next step. Unfortunately, I did not finish the program because a year later, I returned to California as a civilian with a one-year tourist visa to visit friends who had just moved to San Francisco.

My tourist visa ran out but I chose to stay in the U.S. After 18 years as an undocumented immigrant, I got sworn in to become an American citizen in October 2008, with the help of a big-hearted immigration attorney who took my unique, complicated case. The virtue of my military service during wartime with the new immigration laws qualified me for an expedited citizenship given to a small number of immigrants.

I remained stuck for many years pursuing my citizenship with the fear of deportation. What this fundamentally showed me was, when we are in fear, our vision gets hazy and we hesitate to move forward. The Vietnamese monk Thich Nhat Hanh said, "People usually consider walking on water or in thin air a miracle. But I think the real miracle is not to walk either on water or in thin air, but to walk on earth. Every day we are engaged in a miracle which we don't even recognize: a blue sky, white clouds, green leaves, the black, curious eyes of a child—our own two eyes. All is a miracle."

Walking on solid ground, moving forward, breaking through, and exploring possibilities, are all choices we make every day. When we identify a problem and we want to fix it, be ready to make some changes and be flexible. It's also okay not to do anything about a specific situation as long as we move on and quit complaining. No pity party here. Again, it's a choice we make every moment.

Meditation Practice: Active Breathing

1. Lie on your back.
2. Place your right hand on your heart and your left hand on your abdomen.
3. Take a deep breath and allow the lower lungs and abdomen to expand.
4. Then let the air out allowing the abdomen to contract.
5. Each time notice the left hand on the abdomen rise and fall. Next, inhale deeply, and this time, allow the sides of the body to expand along with the abdomen.
6. Then exhale allowing the abdomen to contract again.
7. Lastly, take a deep breath in, allowing the abdomen, sides of the body and the chest to rise.
8. Exhale from the chest to the abdomen.
9. On this last step, notice the right hand rise and fall as you inhale and exhale.
10. Always inhale from the abdomen up and exhale from the collarbone down back to the abdomen. This will ensure that you are breathing deeply.
11. Return to normal breathing.
12. By focusing on the breathing, the mind calms down, allowing you to become present in the moment. Your body gets nutrient-rich oxygen to support the cells and expel waste products in the form of carbon dioxide.

This page is left blank intentionally. You may write your insights and observations on this page or a piece of paper.

CHAPTER SIX

STRENGTHEN CORE VALUES

"A red flower is not red – no flowers have color in the beginning. The color appears and goes as time passes. Likewise, all manifestations in the universe change their appearances from moment to moment. Nothing is permanent." – ***a Japanese quote***

This pose opens the pelvic area that is prone to tightness and tension. Freeing this complex area has a significant effect on the low back, providing a clear path of energy to the spine and the rest of the body. The bones in the pelvis include the sacrum, the tailbone and the hipbones. Major muscle groups include the psoas, gluts, piriformis and adductors. Releasing an aspect of the pelvis area can have a relieving chain reaction on the body. For example, if you feel tingling or poor circulation in your legs, this might be the cause of a tight piriformis pressing on the sciatic nerve from the spine.

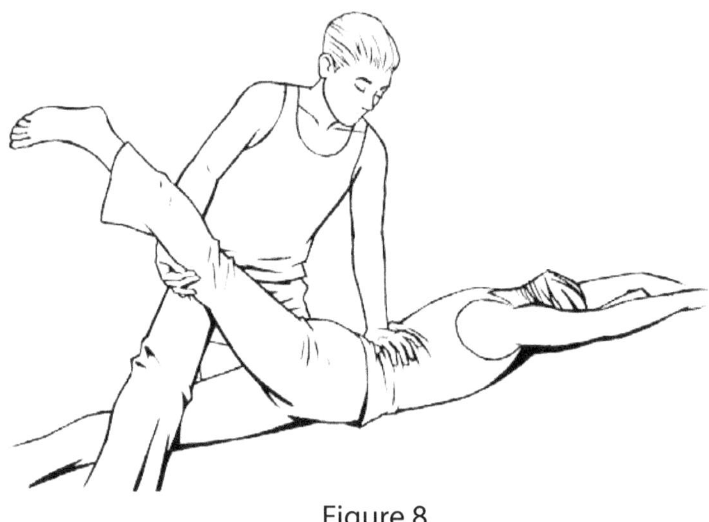

Figure 8

In addition, the health of the pelvis tones up the functioning of the circulatory, digestive, reproductive, and nervous systems.

Yoga Massage Instruction:

1. Giver grabs partner's lower right knee and extends the thigh 45 degrees, opening the hip girdle. The thigh and knee on the ground form a triangle with the straight leg.
2. Giver sits next to bent leg. Palm press thighs and gluts. Note: Be careful not to press on the knees. Pad the bent knee if necessary.
3. Giver uses soft forearm to press the thighs and gluts perpendicularly.
4. Giver uses soft elbow to press deeply around the hipbone and pelvis.
5. Alternate move: Press around hipbones and pelvis area using thumb over thumb.
6. Finish with gentle calming palm presses.
7. Lift whole leg from underneath the knee for support to stretch the quads and hip (*see Fig 8*).

Figure 9

8. Move knee closer to the other knee and bend lower leg up towards the sky.
9. Straddle partner's bent knee and massage foot with palm of hands or elbows (*see Fig 9*).
10. Rotate ankles and toes as you massage the tiny muscles and tendons around ankles and toes using small circular motions.

Awakening the Serpent

I must admit that as a massage therapist, sexual energies can be present between clients and therapists. Opening the pelvic area can trigger pent up emotions. There are legitimate concerns about client's sexual desires. These desires are not necessarily directed to the therapist, but to other people, their partners, or they might be dealing with their own challenges. I address this issue first by being truthful as a healer, and second by shedding light to my clients on ways to find their own needs. I start by doing Reiki[32] energy work starting from their crown chakra down to the groin without physically touching them. I may sense dense energy around the throat—a possible failure to communicate their desires with their partners. Or I may sense a lack of energy located on the solar plexus, which can be interpreted as lack of will power or weakness. By energetically working on the secondary layer of the body, we are able to bring about healing and harmony to both the body and the mind.

There are a number of misconceptions about where the sexual energy comes from. According to *The Chakra Handbook*, "Most people experience sexuality only via the second chakra. In addition, the energy of the root chakra plays a dominant role in the male sex as a physical driving force. If sexuality remains limited to the lower chakras, it becomes rather a unilateral experience which tends to leave both partners weakened and dissatisfied, inclined to separate quickly and go back to being alone again. This is comparable to strumming merely one or two strings of a

---

[32] Reiki is a form of healing using energy and laying of hands on a client. Minimal touch is needed but the effects are nurturing and deep.

musical instrument; the entire spectrum of sounds it is capable of will never ring out."[33]

Many seek massage for pleasure, and some misconstrue these feelings for sexual reasons. There are men and women who get aroused during a session. This is a natural and healthy parasympathetic nervous system response. One should never feel sorry or guilty about it. In case this happens, and it does happen, it is most beneficial for the receiver to move the energy from the groin, along the backside of the body (spine) then returning down the front, back to the groin completing the cycle. A tingling sensation, or mini "orgasms"[34] might be felt throughout the body.

This phenomenon in Tantra is called Kundalini[35] rising, or the awakening of the serpent. The Kundalini is a powerful practice to balance energy for endurance and peak performance that can be useful both in and out of massage sessions. This way, you are in control of your own body. Energy gets contained, reused and circulated until the moment you need it the most.

---

[33] Shalila Sharamon and Bodo J. Baginski, *The Chakra Handbook*

[34] Orgasm is not the same as ejaculation, although some people mistakenly confuse the two.

[35] The Kundalini resides in the sacrum bone in three and a half coils and has been described as a residual power of pure desire, according to Wikipedia.

Meditation Practice: The Middle Way to Meditate

There is a "right" way to meditate, contrary to popular belief. What meditation is not: it is not a way to get you somewhere, because you remain where you are after meditation. Yes it is true that it relaxes your mind and your body, but the grasping of the outcome of the meditation is a deterrent to the actual act of meditation. Remember karma yoga in the introduction? Karma yoga is acting without consideration of personal self-centered desires, likes, or dislikes. So instead of grasping for the outcome, make meditation an act of offering. Be in the present moment. Let things unfold in front of you like a budding lotus blossom.

1. Sit in a comfortable position.
2. Breathe in through the nose, expanding the abdomen and back kidney area.
3. Breathe out through the nose, contracting the abdomen.
4. Do this a few times.
5. If your mind starts to wander, just watch it wander. You don't have to follow the strings of thoughts.
6. You remain steady, unmoved and become an observer of your own thoughts and body.

PART TWO

SUPINE: FACING FATHER SKY

This page is left blank intentionally. You may write your insights and observations on this page or a piece of paper.

CHAPTER SEVEN

OPENING THE HIPS

"The breeze is warm, then a bird sings, breaking through the silence of the forest. One hears the steps of summer approaching..." – ***a Japanese saying***

This step mobilizes the hip joint and helps lubricate the joint with sinovial fluid. Located between the femur and the sacrum, the hip joint supports the weight of the body both in standing, sitting, and walking positions. The major muscles around this area include the gluteus major, medial, minor, piriformis, psoas, and deep hip flexor muscles. As you can see, all these muscles are responsible for the function of the hip joint. Releasing tension in the surrounding muscles through massage or stretching can improve hip stability, posture, and optimum flow of energy into the lower and upper part of the body.

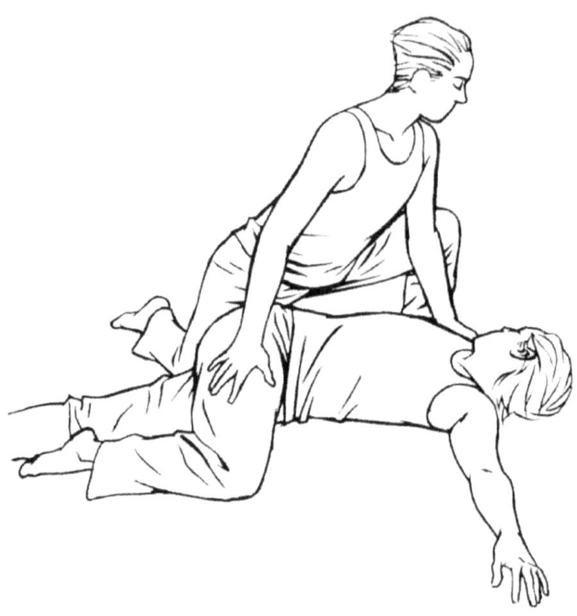

Figure 10

Hot Yoga Tip:

Uttanasana or standing forward bend pose. Stand upright hands on hips. Exhale and bend forward from the hip joints, not from the waist. Do this by aligning your torso, heart, neck and shoulders parallel to the ground as you come halfway down the bend. As you continue, keep the torso wide, open and long without rounding the shoulders and neck. Bend the knees as necessary to keep the back straight and the spine in alignment. Then just let your head, neck and shoulders hang loose as you complete the pose.

Yoga Massage Instructions:

1. Giver kneels with one knee just like making a marriage proposal.
2. Pick up partner's heel with right hand and support the knee with the other hand.
3. Stretch partner's hamstrings by bringing the knee to the chest.
4. Perform hip rotation by moving the knee in circles, like stirring a pot.
5. Make sure giver kneels close to partner to avoid overextending giver's back.
6. Now stretch the low back by bringing the knee over the other leg (*see Fig 10*).

Toning the Skin and Muscles

One of the most important lessons I learned while touching my toes in Uttanasana pose, was to engage the abdomen muscles, and internally rotating my thighs while extending my hips laterally. For a long time I couldn't reach the ground with my fingertips even after months of practice. It was the mental expansion and widening of the hips and lengthening of my back muscles that did the trick. It saved my low back from unnecessary strain, and I began to truly enjoy the pose later on. So once in a while, remind yourself to open your hips, and release the muscles around the gluts. In short, relax and do not have such a tight ass.

To firm up your leg muscles, contain your physical body first by (mentally) hugging your skin to the muscles, then actively squeezing your muscles to the bones. Physiologically, this isometric exercise of muscular contraction against resistance, without significant shortening of muscle fibers, marks an increase in muscle tone.

(If you can't get the leg skin and muscles to contract, start with your arms. Cross your forearms and resist like you're arm wrestling. Maintain the muscle and skin engagement while uncrossing the forearms).

Once you get your foundation and your body contained, do the reverse; relax the muscles away from your bones. And then peel the skin away from your muscles. You'll end up with a stable core and relaxed, soft skin. Do this a few times until you feel the firmness in your skin and muscles.

***The Wild Geese*[36]:**
by American Poet Mary Oliver

You do not have to be good.
You do not have to walk on your knees
for a hundred miles through the desert repenting.
You only have to let the soft animal of your body
love what it loves.

Tell me about despair, yours, and I will tell you mine.
Meanwhile the world goes on.
Meanwhile the sun and the clear pebbles of the rain
are moving across the landscapes,
over the prairies and the deep trees,
the mountains and the rivers.
Meanwhile the wild geese, high in the clean blue air,
are heading home again.

Whoever you are, no matter how lonely,
the world offers itself to your imagination,
calls to you like the wild geese, harsh and exciting —
over and over announcing your place
in the family of things.

Touching the ground with your hands in a standing pose is our "place in the family of things", with a body that is both strong and soft at the same time, free of pain. Mastering this pose brings out your true unmoved engaged nature.

[36] Oliver, M., *Wild Geese, Selected Poems*

Meditation Practice: Sinking Into the Soft Clouds

1. Lie on your back. Feel your toes, the bottoms of your feet, your ankles, with your legs, your knees and your thighs on the ground.
2. Imagine a soft candlelight caressing and warming your feet and your legs until you feel your feet, legs, and body being lifted off the ground.
3. Now imagine your feet, legs, and body sinking to the ground as if you're sinking in soft fluffy clouds.
4. Feel every part of your toes, your feet, every bone and every inch of your skin. Stay present with your legs and thank them for giving you the foundation, strength and support you need every day.

CHAPTER EIGHT

BUILDING A SOLID FOUNDATION

"After working hard during the day, the silence of sitting in the evening can be magnified hundreds of thousands of times. Sitting in Zen meditation in the night is difficult, especially after many hours of hard labor—you get sleepy, get stung by mosquitoes, and delusional thoughts may pass through your mind. Then miraculously, an unexpected wisdom comes. The physical exhaustion had opened your mind." – ***a Japanese quote***

The feet and the legs are the foundation of our body, and when the foundation is weak or too rigid due to tight muscles or unstable joints, it has a direct effect on the spine and the rest of the body.

Making the legs and feet resilient and strong will absorb the shock that the body is subjected to on a daily basis.

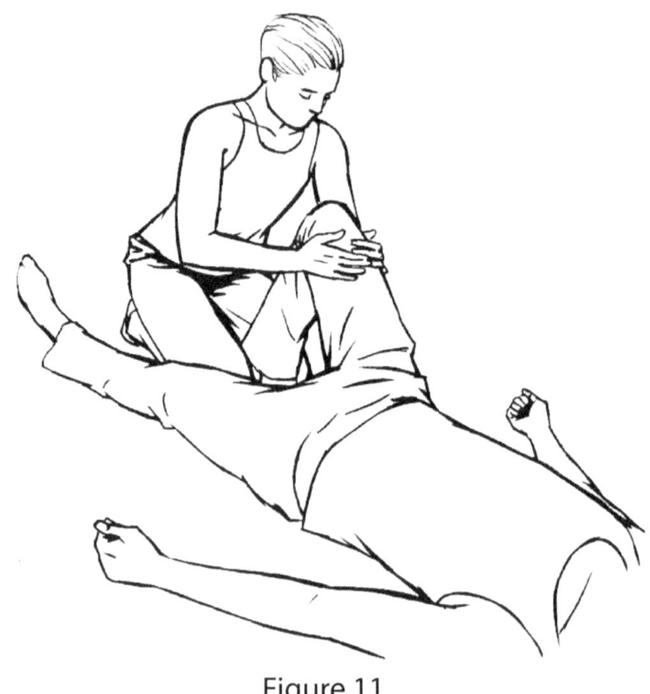

Figure 11

Yoga Massage Instructions:

1. Giver bends the knee toward the ceiling and sits on the floor with the partner's foot between his or her legs (*see Fig 11*).
2. Interlace hands over partner's thighs and compress thighs using the soft pinky edge and pads of the hands. Use your whole body for leverage and pressure.
3. Lean back pulling the thighs toward you and notice your partner's low back being lifted off the mat. This will ease tension in the low back as well.
4. Repeat 2-3 times.
5. Move hands to the back of the calf, this time using the tips of the fingers to separate the calf muscles along the midline. Again use the whole body for leverage and lean back gently if necessary.

Figure 12

6. Giver sits below partner's extended foot and slides his leg underneath his partner's opposite knee from the inside leg (*see Fig 12*).
7. Begin rotating, stretching and squeezing partner's foot, moving your own body gently, as if you two are being rocked in a boat.

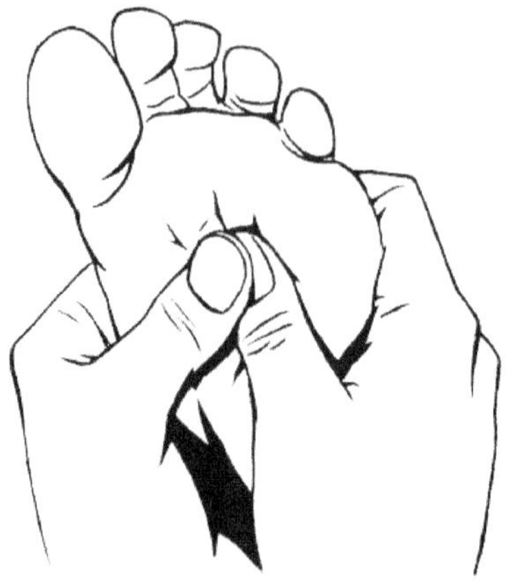

Figure 13

8. Massage bottom of foot using knuckles or supported thumbs starting from the heels up to the toes (*see Fig 13*). Follow the lines between the tarsal and metatarsal[37] bones of the toes.

[37] Bones connecting the toes with the anklebone.

Figure 14

9. Grab both feet and bring them over partner's head. Make sure you maintain your own erect posture preventing strain in the lower back.
10. Receiver places both hands on knees to support legs and experience full stretch from the hamstrings up to the mid back (*see Fig 14*).

THE ART OF STANDING AND SITTING

There's so much to learn about our legs and feet—important body parts that we take for granted. Every time I stand, I always check to be sure where my body is in space and that my foundation is set: the second toe and heel line up parallel, about hip distance apart, the four corners of the foot are planted on the ground with emphasis on the energy flow from the base of the big toe to the inner edge toward the back heel. In this way, my legs and feet are balanced, toned and properly aligned. During the days when I was in the military, we marched and trained for hours and days, but they never taught us the basic mechanics of standing and marching. No wonder a number of injuries relating to the feet, legs, and back were common during training. When you stand up straight, *prana*, or energy rises all the way to the top of your head bringing you closer to the sky. (We are truly the strongest link between the earth and the sky.) However, when we collapse or become too rigid, energy flow gets restricted. That's why it's not a good idea to lock your knees whenever you are standing.

The same principle applies when you sit—make sure your foundation is set: the second toe and heel line up parallel, about hip distance apart, the four corners of the foot are planted on the ground with emphasis on the energy flow from the base of the big toe to the inner edge toward the back heel. Internally rotate the inner thighs from the knee to the buttocks separating the butt cheeks apart. This way you're directly sitting on your sits bone.

Tilt the tailbone and sacrum in (as opposed to out, as we tend to do) releasing tension in the lower back. Then tighten the abdominal muscles to support the low back. This is helpful for people suffering from low back pain, hip misalignment, and shoulder tightness.

Meditation Practice: Walking Meditation

This is a great practice to do when you can't find time to sit down and meditate.

1. Be very aware of the lifting of the thigh, bending the knee, following with the lower leg, flexing of the foot and position of the toes up and back on the ground.
2. Notice where tensions exist in those areas. You don't have to adjust your body, or make judgments—just notice every movement and every sensation in the muscles and joints.
3. Do this in very slow movements—like walking on the moon. You might want to do this at home, at the park, or an area where not many people are around. It does look strange to be walking this slowly, especially in our culture and in a big city where everything moves fast. But it's worth the effort to walk mindfully and smell the roses along the way.

CHAPTER NINE

HELPING HANDS

"Just sit without movement—forget about everything, just sit and meditate. Then someday you will be enlightened." – ***a Japanese quote***

The hands and arms are extensions of the heart. We show our love and warmth by giving someone a big warm hug or a firm handshake. However, modern technology, such as computers, cell phones, and electronic gadgets, build walls and keep our hands and minds distracted. They create tension and conditions that didn't exist before, like carpal tunnel syndrome, tightness on the scalene (neck) muscles, collapsed, rounded shoulders, etc. The promise of technology making our lives easier just got colder. It goes without saying that we are less adept in using our hands to make contact and communicate with other people. No wonder we are so hungry for touch.

We need a revolution to bring touch back into style and make it sexy again. One of my editors ironically commented: "The cell phone is a symbol of modern mankind's inability to communicate".

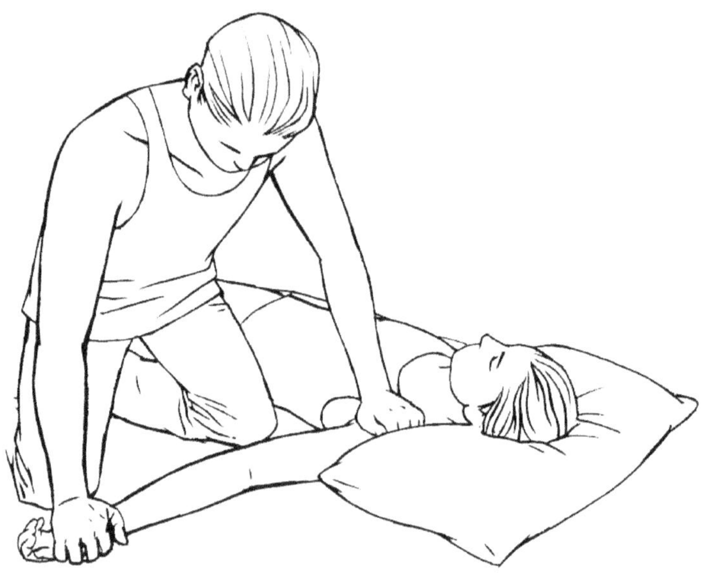

Figure 15

Yoga Massage Instructions:

1. Giver sits at a 90- or 45-degree angle, facing partner's head.
2. Place receiver's arm in front of giver's knees and legs.
3. Anchor hand to receiver's extended hand (*see Fig 15*).
4. Gently press with the palm starting from chest to biceps all the way to the hand, avoiding direct heavy pressure on the shoulder, elbow, and wrist joints.
5. Place receiver's hand between knees.
6. Massage palms of hands and forearms.
7. Interlace fingers between partner's fingers and massage pads of palm with thumb or fingers.
8. Rotate wrists and fingers five times in each direction.
9. Massage each finger joint five times in each direction with thumb.

10. It is optional to use oil or lotion for glide at this point.
11. Take as much time as you can with the hands, as they require much needed attention. Feel and move every bone and ligament.
12. However, givers must also take care of their own needs by sitting comfortably, preventing strain and joining energies together.

Of Big Bang Theory, Gods and Men

The Merriam Webster dictionary defines spark as something that sets off a sudden force. All throughout our lives we have moments of spark that set off dreams, ideas, and inspiration. I remembered mine clearly when I was seven years old coming home from school one afternoon. It was revealed to me through my juvenile mind that if the sun is just one of the billions of stars in the galaxy, there must be another planet or planets capable of sustaining life. I shared this obscure idea with an adult, only to be scowled at and told, "There is only one earth and creation was an act in biblical proportions." That was the end of the conversation.

That incident didn't stop me from feeding my inquisitive mind. In my early 20's, I attended a transformational course in San Francisco that sparked new possibilities for me. I made a declaration at the end of the course for a world of love, wisdom, connectedness, and power.

I created and stepped into a world of a brilliantly sustainable life.

The Greek god Hermes or Roman god Mercury ruled a legendary world. "Hermes was portrayed as a youthful man. On his missions as the messenger of the gods, he wore a traveling hat sometimes with two little wings, and had winged sandals or shoes and carried a caduceus. He invented alchemy; and he subjects alchemical (sometimes sexual) metaphors, the one that fuses the opposites: male and female, metallic and liquid, matter and spirit, cold and fiery, or poison and healing draught."[38] In her book *Gods in*

---

[38] Dr Bolen, J., *Gods in Every Man*

Every Man, Dr Jean Shinoda Bolen traces the inner patterns or archetypes of Roman and Greek gods that shape men's personalities, careers and personal relationships, based on the theory of Carl Jung.

Hermes resonated with me to unite the opposites, a Hermetic seal of some sort forging a world of dreams and ideas, acting as the messenger between the psychic underworld and the mortal world. In the community where I live, I bridge the gap between science and spirituality, between being born in the east and growing up in the west, between tactile massage therapy and studies in psychology.

If you were given a chance to redefine your world, what would you create for yourself? Find an alchemy you can fuse or a spark you can ignite in your relationships at home, in the office, school, friendships or community. Step into an element of your own dreams. You may find that life becomes rich, full of expression, and most of all, wonderfully alive.

Meditation Practice: Self Reiki Meditation

1. Sit in a comfortable position and place both hands side by side, thumb and pinkie finger slightly overlapping over your heart.
2. Feel the energy coming from the center of your hands to your heart. What is the sensation like?
3. Place your hands over your throat, again, hands side by side and fingers slightly overlapping. Notice the sensation in your body. (This self-Reiki healing, by the way is great for relieving sore throats)
4. Place your hands, pinkie to pinkie, over your eyes. Let go of the mind and body. Soften the face, the forehead, eyes, jaws and skin. Go deeply gently.

CHAPTER TEN

THROAT BACK: ALIGNING THE NECK AND SHOULDERS

"When we live single mindedly, by only wanting to be with the source, nothing will matter to us, not even the sun or the moon. As if emptying a bucket of water, let us abandon all attachments, all delusional thoughts and even pride of our accomplishments." ***– a Japanese quote***

We, too, learn from the plant kingdom. I have a houseplant called a philodendron. Its inch-long heart shaped shiny leaves and foot-long vines drape over the small pot placed on my bookshelf. The plant survives well with weekly watering and indirect sunlight. I noticed that trimming the long vines almost to the base and leaving only three or four long vines produces a healthy-looking, lush, vibrant plant. Then a revelation came to me: Reducing the baggage, unnecessary thoughts or chatter, and material effects that make up our lives leads to a more vibrant, lush, and healthy mind and body.

This next pose cuts through illusion, ignorance, and materialism by opening energy channels toward the head, neck, and shoulders.

Keep your head, neck, and shoulders aligned with the source by imagining a plumb line from the central top of the head down to the center of the head between the ears to the soft palate on the mouth. Follow through this plumb line by aligning your head with the center of your heart. Relax into this aligned position without collapsing your head, neck, shoulders, and chest. Notice how your head lifts up to the sky and the heart drops down to the ground. It is effortless and a little awareness of how we hold our neck and shoulders reduces tension in those areas. Think of a houseplant like a philodendron—given proper care, it will seek the light and thrive.

Hot Yoga Tip:

Child's pose is an active resting pose. Sit on your heels, knees hip-width- apart. Keep the toes touching and top of feet on the ground. Bend torso forward leading with your heart, neck, and shoulders while simultaneously engaging the abdomen and leg muscles. Rest the torso on the thighs and place the hands either over your head palms down, or right beside the legs palms up. Make sure the abdomen and legs are engaged to lengthen the low back muscles. See if you can touch your forehead on the ground while keeping the spine, neck, head, and shoulders aligned and not rounded.

Figure 16

Partner Yoga Massage Instructions:

1. Giver assumes a child's pose above the receiver's head. Rise halfway up.
2. Press or lean to partner's shoulders with palm of hands like a cat kneading (yes, you may purr too if you wish).
3. Scoop head with cupped hands and massage occipital with tips of relaxed fingertips using small circular motions (*see Fig 16*).
4. Massage jaw, chin, temples, and scalp with same small circular motions using relaxed fingertips.
5. Giver may deepen the meditation by bending torso forward as in a full child's pose. Both rest while sustaining the connection between the two of you.

A Best Cure for Migraine

I attended a whole day meditation retreat after a New Year's Eve celebration when a headache came up. It was exacerbated when I whiffed lavender from the other side of the meditation room. I tried to get rid of the splitting headache by denying its presence and shoving it down to where I couldn't feel it any longer. I fell asleep during the meditation, only to wake up feeling defeated. You've been there before.

I confronted the pain and investigated the underlying issue. What else would you do while in meditation? I confess my guilt and followed one of the triggers that brought me back to the past and to the exact moment when I had this really intense sensory overload. It was due to some lavender oil I used to cure my own headaches.

I returned to the present and realized that this moment had nothing to do with the past. It was my brain that associated the scent with the past. The olfactory nerve, by the way, links directly to the brain. Only then I was able to make a choice at that very moment to have the headache or not. It's that simple, with practice of course. Obviously, I chose not to have the headache, and the headache was gone.

The various interpretations your mind makes as to how the body may respond to different emotional states represent only possibilities, and are certainly not the only possible reasons for problems of this sort, according to Dr Leon Chaitow, author of *Stress: How to Survive It and Lead a Fuller Life Naturally*. Ask yourself whether your interpretations are accurate or speculative. If not, what do you think might be background reasons contributing to symptoms and signs you are experiencing. When we look at the actual way the body handles strong emotions, both positive and negative, such as fear, anger, and joy, **they are remarkably similar**. Only our mind associates the stimulus and makes possibly faulty conclusions.

Meditation Practice: Breathing Meditation

This is an intense breathing and meditation exercise. Please breathe normally if you find yourself light headed or experience shortness of breath.

1. Sit comfortably on a chair or on a mat.
2. Breathe in, count to three, then breathe out and count to three.
3. Breathe in, count to three, hold the breath (without struggle), count to three, and then breathe out, count to three.
4. Breathe in, count to four, hold the breath, count to four, and then breathe out, count to four. When you hold your breath, find a space of neutrality as if floating in space, yet very grounded at the same time.
5. Continue increasing the number of breaths and holds until you reach ten.
6. Now write down your experience. What did you notice? What was going on with your head while you were doing the exercise?
7. Do you tend to think the same way when you encounter challenging tasks like these in other areas in your life?
8. Notice any tension in your body. Why is there tension?

PART THREE

SEATED: RESTORATIVE POSES

This page is left blank intentionally. You may write your insights and observations on this page or a piece of paper.

CHAPTER ELEVEN

A BEAUTIFUL HEAD

"The thicker the forest, the farther the echo of a monkey's call resounds. When we meditate in a forest, the silence amplifies the slightest sound in nature. The quieter we become, the more we are aware and alert." – ***a poem from 10th century China***

Most of the poses we have done so far involve and integrate the physical body. The next step is to slowly reconnect the mind to the rest of the body. Then slowly return and come back into our physical self—into the "real world" and the family and community in which we serve.

In one of my yoga classes, my teacher Chad Stose mentioned a phenomenon called harmonic entrainment. In physics, this is when a discordant frequency follows a pure wave.

This phenomenon occurs everywhere in the universe. In personal relationships, it is our gravitational pull to people who share our own values, or a dance in unison with someone we love. Some people call it magnetic attraction.

In nature, it is the adaptation and harmony of life to the seasons. We move and live according to the world around us. And in the universal realm, it is the heartbeat of the universe, the primordial sound of OM, we dance to.

On the other hand, as humans, we have "free will"[39] and the capacity to choose for ourselves while taking responsibility for our own actions. Although we follow or entrain ourselves with this pure wave, we just don't respond to this energy but we get to create our own path, and still be with the light. That's the beauty of life. That's a gift we are given to us.

---

[39]There is nothing really free with free will since our choices mostly depends on our history or brain conditioning, in my opinion.

Figure 17

Yoga Massage Instructions:

1. Receiver sits in comfortable cross-legged position.
2. Giver sits behind and with cupped hands massages the neck with fleshy part of palm (see Fig 17).
3. Massage scalp and temples with relaxed fingertips and arms.

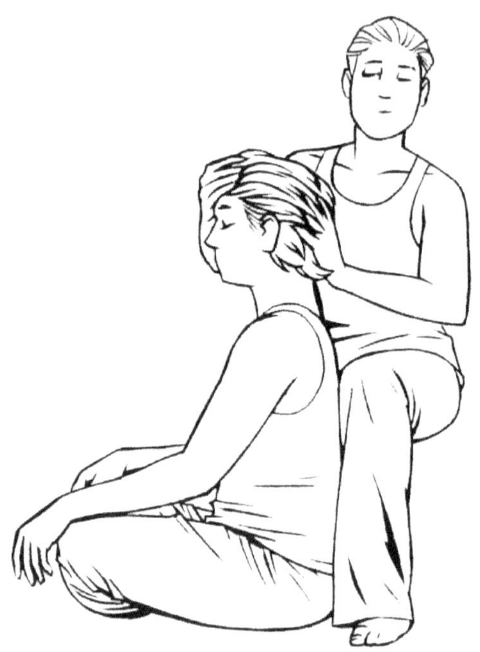

Figure 18

4. Alternative pose: Giver kneels beside partner and holds head with both hands, massaging the scalp and base of head with one hand and anchoring the forehead with the other hand (*see Fig 18*).

WHAT IS THE SOUND OF A BREAKING BOARD IF NO ONE IS AROUND TO HEAR IT?

The sound of a loud kiap[40] and breaking a 10x12x1 piece of board with my closed fist both excites and terrifies me. I feel like this is one of the rites of passage for a Tae Kwon Do martial artist. It is the progression from the militaristic order of practicing and performing the forms, such as marching in place with punches and kicks, to a mind-bending skill of breaking through a solid wooden object with one's bare hand, foot, or head.

Most of you might say it either looks easy or hard to break a board, unless you've done it yourself. Well it's both. There are many factors involved: how dense the board is, how determined you are in breaking a somewhat easy small target, how forceful you are in following through the motion, and most of all, the fear of knowing that there could be physical pain or letting of blood involved in the process. Having the class and instructor behind you in demonstrating this task can be either very helpful or nerve wracking.

[40] Kiap is the sound martial artists use to execute a controlled force such as a kick or a punch.

It is much the same in life, on the yoga mat, and on the massage table, excluding the bloodletting part. There's some point in your practice once you've gone through the motions where you feel like going to the next level of commitment.

After going through the physical movement and teaching your own body to be more comfortable with your partner's body, you become ready to plunge into more powerful energetic levels. Then, your work becomes deep and fulfilling.

Meditation Practice: Compassionate Meditation

1. Sit comfortably on a mat or a chair.
2. Imagine yourself breaking though a difficult situation you'd like to resolve.
3. Think of the end result first—how you see yourself and how it feels in your body to solve this problem. Refuse the temptation to count the material benefits you would get out of this issue, especially if it has something to do with a person or a group of people. Pause. Then allow the thoughts to return to your heart, and give yourself lots of love and compassion. Feel it in your body.
4. Sit for a few moments to breathe deeply in and out, and really sink into your open, spacious heart.
5. Don't even think of how you're going to get there. Just let your heart slowly guide you through. Your heart has the intelligence to heal itself.

This page is left blank intentionally. You may write your insights and observations on this page or a piece of paper.

CHAPTER TWELVE

CHILDREN OF THE LIGHT

"Pure rays from a full moon embrace everything on the land—everyone is given universal compassion at all times, but we do not notice it, do we? It is up to us whether we can shine our inner light by receiving this gift." – ***a Japanese proverb***

This chapter is about getting our needs met. Our basic physical needs according to Maslow[41] are food, water, clothing, shelter and sex. Emotionally, our needs are the sense of safety, security, freedom, and love. Spiritually, whatever our religious practices, we all have common needs: to connect to a larger reality or truth, to answer our calling in life, and to find strength or forgiveness from a supreme entity. This last pose reveals a fundamental truth that, as humans, we do have needs, and yet nature unconditionally provides the rest for us.

41 American Psychologist Abraham Maslow's hierarchy of human needs.

For example, the air we breathe, the water we drink, the ground we walk upon, gravity, sunlight, nighttime, seasons, food on our table (even though we buy these things), natural resources, other plants and animals, are nature's gifts that we sometimes take for granted, neglect, or abuse.

Figure 19

Yoga Massage Instructions:

1. From the previous pose, receiver sits in comfortable cross-legged position, while giver sits behind.
2. Receiver interlaces fingers behind neck, while giver grabs both biceps, leans back and stretches partner's shoulders, back, and opens up the chest, side ribs, and heart area (*see Fig 19*). Offer your heart to the light.
3. Hold for a few breaths; then repeat twice.
4. Alternate move: from the seated position, both giver and receiver slightly twist to the left or right by turning the receiver's torso either direction. Go deeper each time you twist.

It's all Relative

Many of us have heard of Albert Einstein's special theory of relativity, but most of us don't understand its significance. This simple and beautiful equation sums up one of the most powerful truths in the universe, according to a BBC[42] documentary. Let's look at the equation:

$$E=mc^2$$

Where: ***E = energy, m = mass****, and* ***c = speed of light***

It basically means that a large amount of energy is equivalent to mass[43] times the square of the speed of light. The speed of light, a physical constant, is 300,000 km/sec, or 186,000 miles/sec. The square of the speed of light is, well, a very large number. It is quite incomprehensible to human perception and reality. This energy goes beyond the law of attraction. In fact, scientists, astronomers, and physicists have used this once illusive theory to measure the distances between stars and galaxies, for GPS navigation, to study quantum physics, and to manufacture nuclear atomic reactors.

Energy = mass (light energy)

So how do we weave this esoteric equation into our practical daily lives and our healing? Pause for a moment, and take this inside your heart. Our physical bodies are made up of atoms or particles that carry mass (m), the same atoms and particles as everything around us all across the universe. The electrons in atoms vibrate at a certain frequency or wavelength and exhibit the same wave

---

[42] British Broadcasting Corporation

[43] Mass is not the same as weight. Weight is relative to gravity.

characteristic as light (c). Therefore, all things in the universe have the characteristic of light—both within the light spectrum and beyond. In short, we are all light beings. Therefore, applying Einstein's theory, if our collective body is light, then it is a potential storehouse of power, wealth, health, vitality, and energy. We just need to know how to plug it in, turn on the switch, engage the wheels, and harness this unlimited gift nature provides for us.

Since we are essentially made up of light particles, we can either swim in it or be blinded by it and not see the light at all. In every science experiment, results vary relative to the position of the observer. When we become the observer of our own self, i.e., our thoughts, emotions, ego, and physical structure, we see a defined body, matter, or mass (m). Then our brain makes associations, judgments, or limitations as to what this self is, i.e., fat, thin, pretty, ugly, happy, sad, failure, etc. Our mind, which is made of matter itself, restricts it's own potential. We therefore can't see our own light.

However, if an observer (you) is not observing this body, everything becomes potentiality, a wave function, or light[44]. Our bodies and surroundings vibrate at different intensities and amplitudes. In this state of spaciousness or consciousness possibilities exist. In this realm of possibilities, light (we) can travel far, fast, forward, back, attract, repel, collapse, expand, bend, and exist synchronously and simultaneously. These are all the potential of light. These are all the potential of our being and existence. Therefore, if we can roll back time, the process of anti-aging is quite possible at this moment.

---

[44] I interchange wave and light here because light is a form of wave. Wave, however, can be electro-magnetic, electrical, power, potential energy, thermal, pulse, vibration, etc.

What arises and cuts through the core of our existence is a genetic composition with **both** particle and wave characteristics existing simultaneously. We bypass all layers of ego, emotions, speech, culture, ethnicity, religious belief, background, shape, texture, color, and everything that we consider our "reality." Zoom deeper into the cellular level. As humans we have the advantage and the capacity **by power of choice** to behave as a particle or wave, or both. We have the willpower to let go of the illusions that restrict our growth, hinder our healing, add to our suffering, or make our energies discordant causing dis-eases.

Therefore, in every given moment we bounce off between particle and light. It's simple—if it weighs you down you're behaving like a particle—if it's uplifting you're beaming like a light. Instantaneously, you get to choose how to exist in this world.

So every morning, when I wake myself from sleep, I check in with myself to see where I am in space. I then create possibilities for myself—be it abundance, compassion, wisdom, equanimity, or whatever. I send this energy out to the universe and allow the universe to bounce it back to me in one form or the other. I just switch on my body and mind's **light** function and let my day begin. On any given day we can choose to create or react to our environment. I choose to create.

Another example is my habit of running late to my coaching appointments. One day, the morning I was to turn in my book manuscript, I was doing last minute changes, and I left my apartment a few minutes later than I had anticipated. I didn't want to be late again, so I switched on my wave function, and projected my body and my mind at our meeting place "on time." Meanwhile, I called a cab to pick me up, walked out my front door, hopped in the cab, and inserted the last-minute changes I made into the finished manuscript during the cab ride. The whole trip I was efficient, calm, and flowed like a wave of infinite possibility. I got to our meeting place a few minutes ahead of time, confident, secure, and stress free.

You don't have to be an Einstein to be a genius. Remember, the mind is a terrible thing to waste, and so is the body. Live as a light being now—free—in tune with the cycle of the universe. Turn your mind into light energy and reach your full potential.

The energy around matter is so powerful it can overcome perceived limitations. As Einstein himself puts it, "I am enough of an artist to draw freely upon my imagination. Imagination is more important than knowledge. Knowledge is limited. Imagination encircles the world."

Time in a Bottle

A quick note about time, as we seem to stress about it all the "time." We use time as an industrial tool to synchronize our work and lives, or as an excuse for our limitations. In fact, time is a product of the industrial revolution of the 1850s. In effect, we've become slaves to time—we always run out of time, we run late, we're too old, we're afraid of dying, etc. Remember the basic needs list in the beginning of the chapter? Is time on that list? It is not—because time is merely a tool and a concept.

As a generalization and personal theory using Einstein's equation:

$$\mathbf{E=mc2}$$

Where: E = energy, m = mass, and c = speed of light.

When we replace "time" with zero, as in right now, not the industrial mechanical time as in 12:35 PM, but this moment at zero point, at rest:

$$\mathbf{E=kilogram\ (meter/second)^2 = \frac{kilogram\ (meter)^2}{0}}$$

The resulting Energy is infinite[45].

For a moment, freeze this infinite time and step into an infinite space. Close your eyes. What do you feel,see, and hear? What are the infinite possibilities that is happening at this moment? In this empty infinite state, create your possibilities – it is happening in this moment. It is powerful, isn't it?

---

[45]Mathematically, any number divided by zero is infinite.

Time in reality is the beating of your own heart. Listen to it. Let your mind drop down to meet your heart in perfect balance and harmony with your whole body. And be the light to other people, beings, and the whole of the universe. **Shine. Live. Be free now!**

Meditation Practice: Guiding Light Meditation

1. Sit comfortably on a chair or mat.
2. Silently make intent or think of a word (for example: love, compassion, truth, healing, power, wisdom, etc) or a name (for example: a person, animal companion, teacher, a guru, or someone you look up to). As a side note, *gu* in Sanskrit literally means darkness and *ru* means light, *guru*[46] therefore means the one who brings darkness into light. Another definition is "the weighty one," or widely used meaning "the teacher." Using our previous theory, all of us are gurus having the same properties with physical mass (m) and the ability to generate light energy (c).
3. Imagine that word or name as a small light (try not to associate this word or person with a feeling or description, just be with an energy) coming from the center of your forehead.
4. Now drop this light into your heart and fill your heart space with the energy and let this energy attach itself to every cell and mass in your being.
5. Pause for a few moments.
6. Stop here if you feel complete.
7. If you are feeling overwhelmed, tense, or upset, you may also freely reverse the process by gathering this energy from the cells and fusing them into one small manageable mass.
8. Send this particle to the crown of your head and offer it to the universe as a way of "recycling" the energy. Whenever you are ready you may let go of this energy. Need I say energy is a terrible thing to waste?

---

[46] Guru, or *guro* in the Philippine and Indonesian language means teacher.

9. Another way to recycle energy is to turn it the other direction and send it to your solar plexus. Use this particle to boost your energy level as a storehouse of power, passion, or creativity.
10. Or, you may bounce off from top to bottom, from the crown of your head to the solar plexus, and sift though energies you want to let go or keep.
11. Remember the property of waves—there is the potential to travel far, fast, forward, back, attract, repel, collapse, bend, expand, and exist synchronously and simultaneously.
12. Finally, if you're still feeling overwhelmed, tense, or upset, remember you are the observer of your own thoughts and emotions. This is an energy that weighs you down. Consider switching from particle to light function and notice how your body or mind changes. If you find some things that are easy and fast to bring you down, it's as easy and fast to pick yourself up. Nothing is permanent—you have the power to make changes in each moment. And each moment presents itself with an infinite number of possibilities.

This page is left blank intentionally. You may write your insights and observations on this page or a piece of paper.

EPILOGUE

"There is no passion to be found in playing small—in settling for a life that is less than the one you are capable of living."
- Marianne Williamson

All forms of art whether fine art, music, dance, or writing, are produced not only to express an artist's creativity and response ability, but also to let the audiences get lost in dreams, fantasies, or memories. Our own truths, experiences and connections make us feel whole, complete, and be in synch with the world. And yet, as humans, our five senses are programmed to grasp for more and something solid, outside our own limitations.

Appreciate what is given to us—our sense of sight, hearing, touch, thoughts, or life itself, rather than grasping for material things or hopes that give us a false sense of happiness.

The artist, then, creates art for the purpose of entertainment or grandiosity for himself and for his audience. He creates a medium for connection, fulfillment, longing, and awakening for other people. Now that's a weighty (*guru*) proposition—for a single person to make a difference with a "light" contribution to all of mankind. – Errol

EXPLORE MORE

For more information about the book, workshops, events, and updates please visit us at:

www.ensocircle.com.

Please keep us in touch. Send communications and feedback to:

Enso Circle Media
2370 Market St #155,
San Francisco, Ca 94114
(415) 552-5524

Join Facebook group:
yoga_massage_book group

How to Order

To order this book or others, visit Amazon.com.

Thank you.

THE 12 POSES[47]

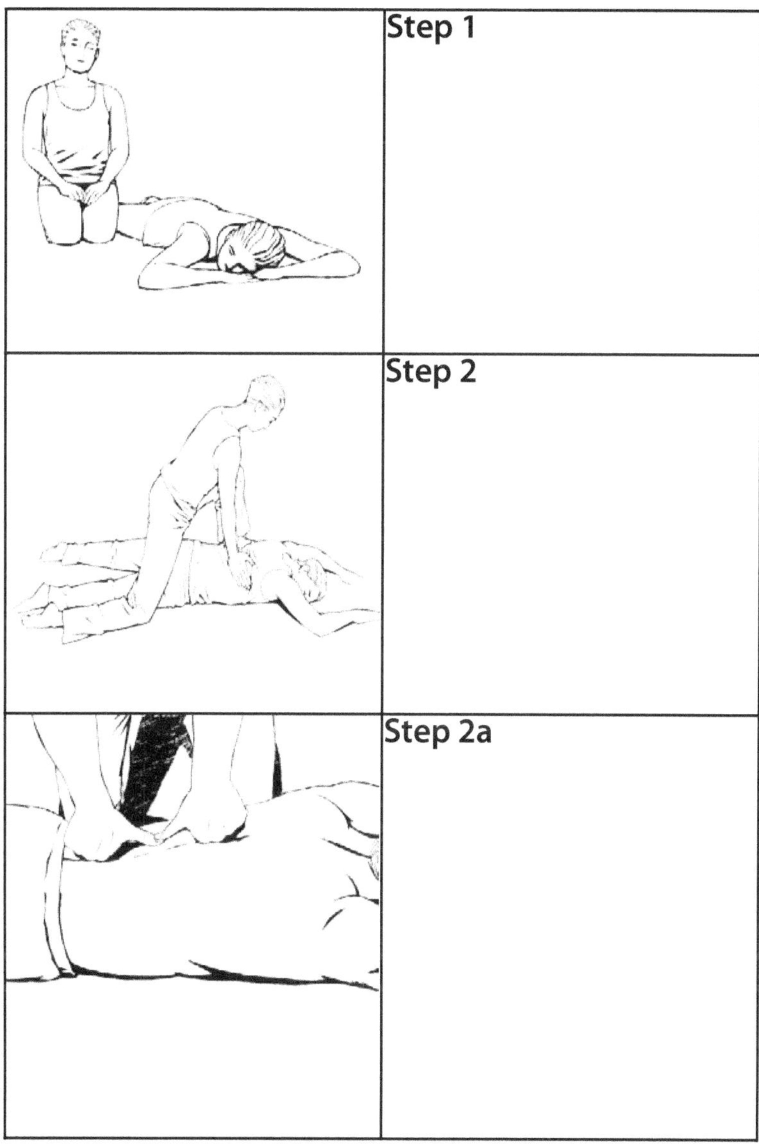

	Step 1
	Step 2
	Step 2a

[47] Previous first step on each page are repeated as guides.

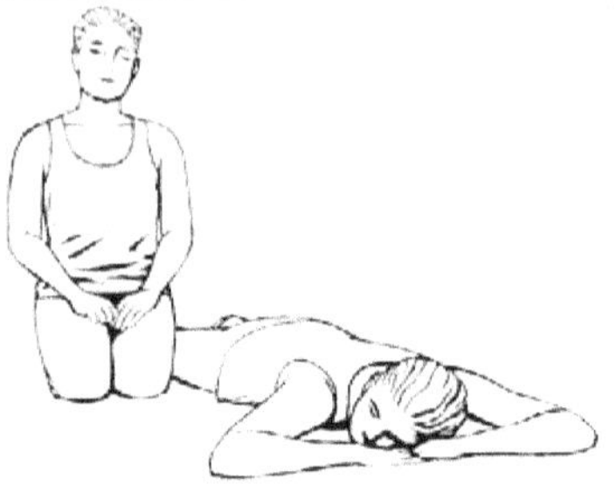	Step 1
	Step 3

	Step 4
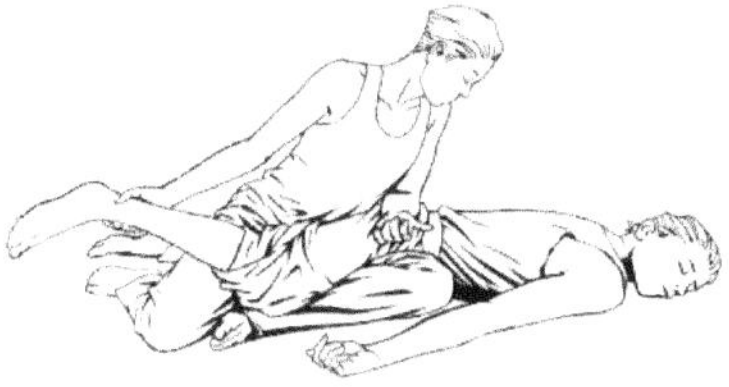	Step 5
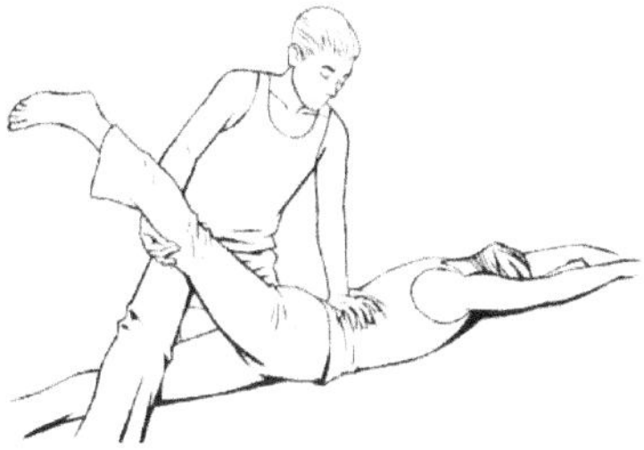	Step 6

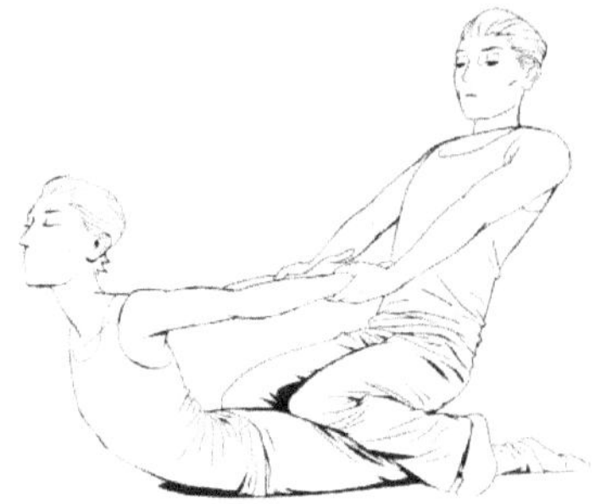	Step 4
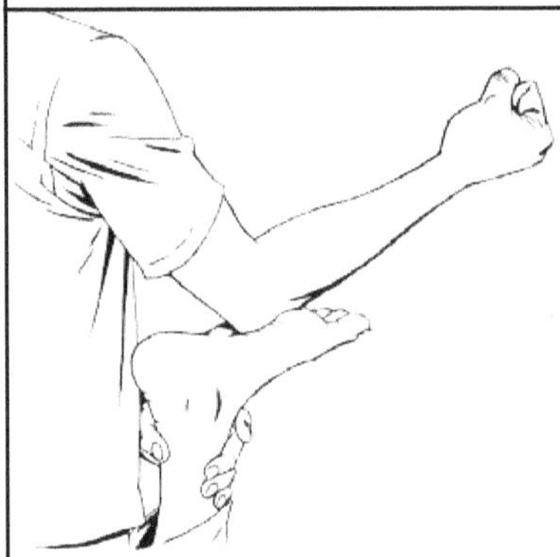	Step 6a

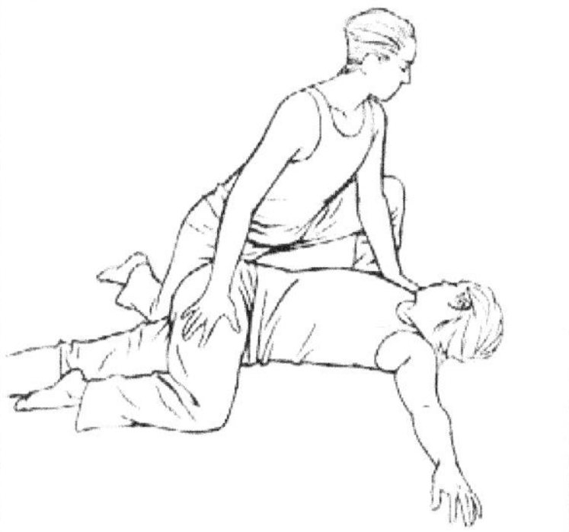	**Step 7**
	**Step 8**
	**Step 8a**
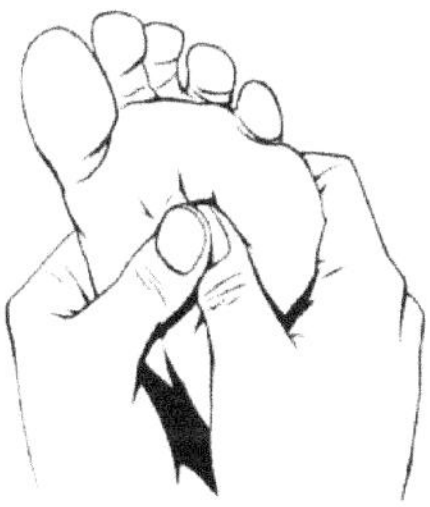	**Step 8b**

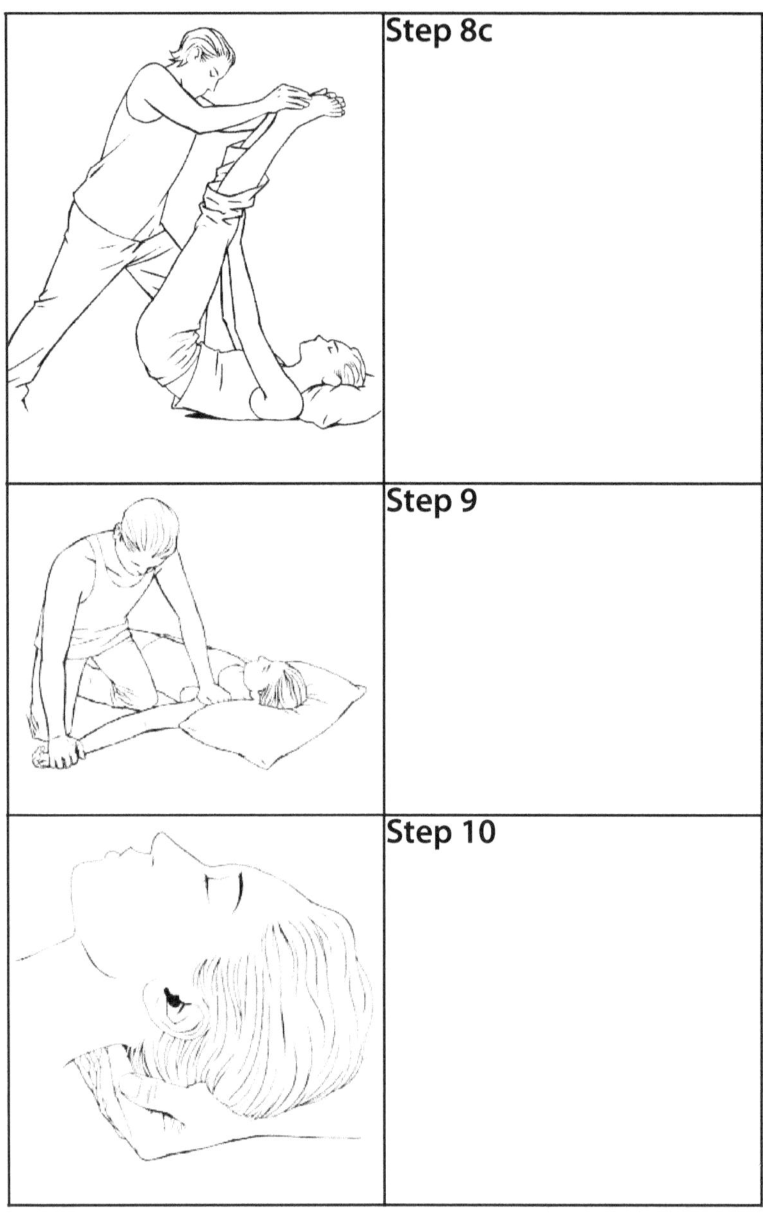
Step 8c
Step 9
Step 10

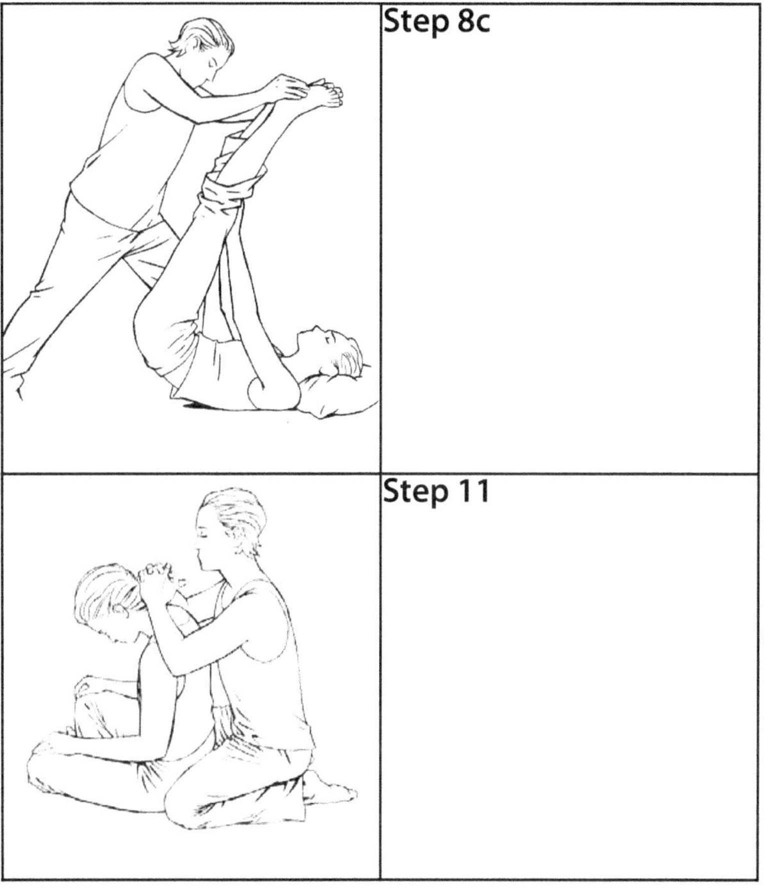

Step 8c

Step 11

Step 11a
Step 12

Notes:

www.ingramcontent.com/pod-product-compliance
Lightning Source LLC
LaVergne TN
LVHW020632100826
845148LV00012B/2143

9780615382302